RUTHLESS MAGNATE, CONVENIENT WIFE

BY
LYNNE GRAHAM

D0318303

 MILLS & BOON®

First published in Great Britain 2009
Harlequin Mills & Boon Limited,
Eton House, 18-24 Paradise Road, Richmond, Surrey TW9 1SR

© Lynne Graham 2009

ISBN: 978 0 263 87753 3

Set in Times Roman 10½ on 12¾ pt
01-0110-49163

Harlequin Mills & Boon policy is to use papers that are natural, renewable and recyclable products and made from wood grown in sustainable forests. The logging and manufacturing process conform to the legal environmental regulations of the country of origin.

Printed and bound in Spain
by Litografia Rosés, S.A., Barcelona

RUTHLESS MAGNATE, CONVENIENT WIFE

CHAPTER ONE

OIL billionaire, Sergei Antonovich, travelled behind tinted windows in a big black glossy four-wheel drive. Two car-loads of bodyguards flanked him, in front and behind. Such a sight was worthy of note en route to a remote Russian village like Tsokhrai. But everyone who saw the cavalcade pass knew exactly who it was, for Sergei's grandmother was well known locally, and her grandson always visited her on Easter Day.

Sergei was looking at the road that he had turned from a dirt track into a broad highway to facilitate the transportation needs of the coach-building factory he had set up to provide employment in this rural area. In the winters, when once he had lived here, the road had been thick with mud and often impassable by anything more sophisticated than a farm cart. When it had snowed, the village had been cut off for weeks on end. Sometimes even Sergei still found it hard to believe that he had spent several years of his adolescence in Tsokhrai, where he had suffered the pure culture shock of an urban tearaway plunged into a rustic nightmare of clean country living. At the age of thirteen, he had been six feet tall, a gang member and embryo thug, accus-

tomed to breaking the law just to survive. His grandmother, Yelena, had been barely five feet tall, function-
ally illiterate and desperately poor. Yet Sergei knew that
everything he had become and everything he had
achieved in the years since then was down to the inde-
fatigable efforts of that little woman to civilise him.

The convoy came to a halt outside a humble building clad in faded clapboards and sheltering behind an
overgrown hedge. The bodyguards, big tough men who
wore sunglasses even on dull days and never smiled,
leapt out first to check out the area. Sergei finally
emerged, a sartorial vision of elegant grooming in a silk
and mohair blend suit that was superbly tailored to his
broad-shouldered powerful physique. His ex-wife,
Rozalina, had called this his 'annual guilt pilgrimage'
and had refused to accompany him. But his visit was
enough reward for the elderly woman who would not
even let him build her a new house. Yelena, Sergei reflected grimly, was the only female he had ever met
who wasn't eager to take him for every ruble she could
get. He had long since decided that extreme greed and
an overriding need to lionise over others were essen-
tially feminine failings.

As Sergei strode down the front path towards the
dwelling, villagers fell back from where they were gathered in its doorway and an awe-inspired silence fell.
Yelena was a small plump woman in her seventies with
bright eyes and a no-nonsense manner. She greeted him
without fuss, only the huskiness of her voice and her use
of the diminutive name 'Seryozh' for him hinting at
how much her only grandchild meant to her.

'As always you are alone,' Yelena lamented, guiding

him over to the table, which was spread with a feast of food to satisfy those who had just finished practising a forty-day fast in honour of the season. 'Eat up.'

Sergei frowned. 'I haven't been—'

His grandmother began to fill a large plate for him. 'Do you think I don't know that?'

The bearded Orthodox priest sitting at the table, which was decorated with flowers and painted eggs, gave the younger man who had rebuilt the crumbling church tower an encouraging smile. 'Eat up,' he urged.

Sergei had skipped breakfast in anticipation of the usual gastronomic challenge that awaited him. He ate with appetite, sampling the special bread and the Easter cake. Throughout, he was approached by his grandmother's visitors and he listened patiently to requests for advice, support and money, because he was also the recognised source of philanthropy in the community.

Yelena stood by watching and concealing her pride. She was wryly aware that her grandson was the cynosure of attention for every young woman in the room. That was understandable: his hard-boned dark features were strikingly handsome and he stood six feet three inches tall with the lean powerful build of an athlete. As always, however, Sergei was too accustomed to female interest to be anything other than indifferent to it. His grandmother had a fleeting recollection of the lovelorn girls who had dogged his every step while he was still a boy. Nothing had changed; Sergei still enjoyed an extraordinary level of charisma.

Sergei was mildly irritated by his female audience and wondered how much Yelena had had to do with the surprising number of attractive well-groomed young women milling about. His concentration, however, had only to alight on his grandmother, though, for it to occur to him that she looked a little older and wearier every time he saw her. He knew she was disappointed that he had failed to bring a girl home with him. But the women who satisfied his white-hot libido in his various homes round the world were not the type he would have chosen to introduce to a devout old lady. He recognised that she was desperate to see him marry and produce a family. It would have surprised many, who saw Sergei solely as an arrogant, notoriously cold-blooded businessman, to learn that he actually believed that he *owed* it to Yelena to give her what she wanted.

After all these years, what thanks had Yelena yet reaped from taking a risk on her once foul-mouthed and defiant grandson? While her guardianship had turned Sergei's life and prospects around, life for her had remained very tough. His immense wealth and success meant virtually nothing to her, yet he was her only living relative. Her husband had been a drunk and a wife-beater, her son had been a car thief and her daughter-in-law an alcoholic.

'You worry about Yelena,' the priest noted sagely. 'Bring her a wife and a grandchild and she will be happy.'

'If only it were so easy as you make it sound,' Sergei quipped, averting his gaze from the excess of cleavage on display as a nubile beauty hurried forward to pour him another coffee.

'With the right woman it *is* that easy!' The priest laughed with the pride and good humour of a family man who had six healthy children.

But Sergei harboured a deep abiding aversion to the

matrimonial state. Rozalina had proved to be a very expensive mistake. And, more significantly, even a decade after the divorce he could not forget the child she had aborted to protect her perfect body. He had never told Yelena about that, as he had known it would have broken her heart and troubled her dreams. He also knew, noting the depth of the lines on her creased and weathered face, that she was on the slippery slope of life and that time was of the essence. Some day there would be no one left to tell him that the noise of his helicopter landing nearby had traumatised her pig and stopped her hens laying. It was a bleak thought that made his conscience stab him. Who had done more for him and who had he rewarded least? If any woman deserved a bouncing baby on her lap, it was Yelena Antonova.

Sergei was still mulling over the problem that afternoon when his grandmother asked him if he ever ran into Rozalina. He managed not to wince. He was a loner, he always had been, and he found personal relationships a challenge. He loved the cut and thrust of business, the exhilaration of a new deal or takeover, the challenge of cutting out the dead wood and increasing profit in the under-performers, the sheer satisfaction of making a huge financial killing. If only marriage could be more like business with clear-cut rules and contracts that left no room for misunderstandings or errors!

An instant later, his high-powered brain kicked up a gear and he thought, *Why not?* Why the hell shouldn't he choose a wife and get a child by the same means in which he did business? After all, trying to do it the old-fashioned way had been catastrophic.

'Is there anyone?' Yelena asked with a guilty edge that told him she had been holding back on that question about his private life all day.

'Perhaps,' he heard himself say, holding out a thread of hope or possibly a foundation for a future development.

And, that fast, the plan began forming. This time around, Sergei decided, he would take the professional practical approach to the institution of marriage. He would draw up a list of requirements, put his lawyers in charge and urge them to use a doctor and a psychologist to weed out unsuitable applicants for the role he envisaged. Of course the marriage would be short-term and he would retain custody of the child. He immediately grasped the dichotomy of his preferences. He didn't want a wife who would do anything for money, but he *did* want one prepared to give him a child and then walk away when he had had enough of playing happy families for Yelena's benefit. But somewhere in the world his perfect matrimonial match had to exist, Sergei reasoned. If he was specific enough with his requirements he would not even have to meet her before the wedding. Energised by that prospect, and once back behind the privacy of the tinted windows of his four-by-four, he began to make bullet points on his notebook computer.

When Alissa saw her sister, Alexa, climbing out of a totally unfamiliar fire-engine-red sports car, she was filled with a lively mix of exasperation, bewilderment and impatience. Even so, a strong thread of relief bound all those disparate emotions together and she hurtled downstairs, a tiny slender blonde with a mass of silvery pale hair and clear aquamarine eyes.

She flung open the front door of the cottage and the questions just erupted from her in a breathless stream. 'Where have you been all these weeks? You promised you'd phone and you didn't! I've been worried sick about you! Where on earth did that fancy car come from?'

Amusement gleaming in her eyes, Alexa strolled forward. 'Hi, twin, nice to see you too.'

Alissa hugged her sister. 'I was going out of my mind with worry,' she admitted ruefully. 'Why didn't you phone? And what happened to your mobile phone?'

'It broke and I got a new number.' Alexa wrinkled her nose. 'Look, things got very complicated and I kept on deciding to wait until I had something more concrete to offer you—and then when I finally *did* have it, I thought it would be easier to just come home and tell you face to face.'

Alissa stared at her sister, not understanding and not expecting to, either. It had always been that way because, although the girls had been born identical, it had been clear from an early age that below the skin they were two very different personalities. Alexa had always been the single-minded, ambitious one, quick to fight and scrap for what she wanted, and she made enemies more easily than she made friends. Alissa was quieter, steadier, occasionally tormented by an overdeveloped conscience and altogether more thoughtful. At twenty-three years of age, the sisters were less obviously twins than they had been as children. Alexa wore her long silvery blonde hair sleek, layered and shoulder length while Alissa's was longer and more usually confined in a ponytail. Alexa wore fashionable, often provocative clothing and revelled in the attention men awarded her, while Alissa dressed conservatively and froze like a rabbit in headlights when men homed in on her more understated charms.

'Where's Mum?' Alexa asked, flinging her coat down in a heap and walking into the kitchen.

'She's at the shop. I came home this afternoon to do the accounts,' Alissa confided, putting the kettle on to boil. 'I gather you got a job in London.'

Alexa gave her a rather self-satisfied smile and leant back against the kitchen counter. 'Of course I did. I'm a whizz at selling luxury cars and I've earned a lot of commission. How's Mum?'

Alissa pursed her lips. 'As good as she's ever going to be. At least I don't hear her crying at night any more—'

'She's getting over it? About time,' Alexa pronounced with approval.

Alissa sighed. 'I don't think Mum's ever really going to get over it—particularly not while Dad's parading his fancy piece round the village. Or with all this debt still hanging over her, not to mention having to sell her home into the bargain...'

Alexa gave her a wide smile. 'Well, I was going to ask you whether you wanted the good or the bad news first. On the way here I stopped off at the solicitor's and told him to go ahead and agree a financial settlement for the house. I also gave him enough money to settle the bills. Prepare yourself for a surprise: I've got the cash to pay off our bastard of a father!'

'Don't talk about Dad like that,' Alissa said uneasily while she struggled to accept the dramatic assurance that the other woman had just voiced. 'Although I agree with the sentiment.'

'Oh, don't be so mealy-mouthed!' Alexa urged tartly. 'Mum loses her son and my boyfriend in a ghastly accident, nurses Dad through his cancer scare and what's her reward? Dad takes off with a hairdresser young enough to be his daughter!'

'You just said you've got enough money to pay off Dad and more for the bills—how is that possible? You've only been away three months.' Alissa was frowning. She wanted so badly to believe it was possible, but her native wit was telling her that even though Alissa was a terrific sales-woman she still didn't have that kind of earning power.

'You could say that I went for a new job with a big cash payment up front. As I said, there's enough to settle all Mum's bills and pay off Dad,' Alexa repeated, keen to make that salient point again.

Alissa was wide-eyed with disbelief. 'As well as enough to buy that car outside *and* renew your designer wardrobe?'

Alexa's smile evaporated as she gave her twin a cool accusing scrutiny. 'You've already noticed the label on my new coat?'

'No, it just has that look. That sophisticated look that expensive clothes always seem to have,' Alissa advanced ruefully. 'What kind of a job pays that much money?'

'Didn't you hear what I told you?' Alexa demanded thinly. 'I've saved our bacon—I have enough money to sort out *all* Mum's problems and give her back her self-respect and security.'

'That would take a miracle.' Alissa was convinced that her sister was wildly exaggerating the case.

'In today's world, you have to compete and work *very* hard and make sacrifices to bring about a miracle.'

At that reference to making sacrifices from a young woman who had never demonstrated the smallest leaning in that direction, Alissa stole a troubled glance at her sister. 'I don't understand.'

'As I said, it's complex. For a start I'm afraid I had to sort of *borrow* your identity.'

Alissa froze at that announcement. 'Borrow my identity? *How?*'

'You're the one with the university degree and I needed to use it on my application to meet the criteria,' Alexa revealed, lifting her chin in defiance of her twin's shaken stare. 'And because I had used it to make myself look educated I had to use your name as well. When they checked out my claims they'd soon have discovered that I was lying if I'd applied under my own name.'

Alissa was very shocked at her sister's casual attitude to what she had done. 'But that's…that's fraud, cheating…'

Alexa's indifference to what she clearly saw as a minor detail was striking. 'Whatever. I thought it was worth a try and so it proved, but then I started seeing someone.'

'You're dating again?' Alissa gasped in surprise and excitement. After her sister's boyfriend, Peter, had died in the same car crash that had taken their brother's life—a tragedy that had soon been followed by their father's shocking defection—Alexa had become so angry and bitter that she had sworn off all men. Alissa had understood the level of her sister's heartbreak for, as their next-door-neighbours' son, Peter had been as much a part of their lives as any member of the family.

'Were you too busy looking at the coat to notice

this?' Alexa extended a hand on which an opulent ruby and diamond ring glowed on her engagement finger.

Alissa gaped. 'You're engaged...*already?*'

'And preggers,' Alexa confided.

'Pregnant as well?' Alissa stared as her sister turned sideways but it was evidently early days for her stomach still looked perfectly flat. 'My word, and you never said a thing about all this until now?'

Alexa grimaced. 'I told you that things had got complicated. I was in the running for that job and I didn't want to tell Harry about it...yes, that's *his* name. He's quite well off—a gentleman farmer who runs his family estate. They're thrilled about me and the baby, not a bit bothered that I'm not one of the county set. But neither he nor his family would understand what I signed up for before we met...or that I could have accepted all that money for the right reasons.'

Her smooth brow furrowing, Alissa stared. 'Alexa, what are you talking about? This job? What money did you accept?'

Alexa sat down at the kitchen table and sipped her tea before she replied. 'I never thought I'd get it. I went through the whole application process out of curiosity. Strictly speaking, it's not really a job,' she admitted in an undertone.

Alissa sank down into the chair opposite. 'Then what is it? It isn't anything, well...immoral, is it?'

'Before I tell you, you think very carefully about what that money will do for Mum,' her sister urged sharply. 'It's her only hope of rescue and I've already paid out most of it on her behalf. All I had to do to get it was agree to marry a very rich Russian and act like his wife.'

'But why would any man want to pay you for doing that? These days I thought most rich Russians were beating off gold-digging women with sticks,' Alissa remarked drily.

'This guy wants it all done on a business basis, with money paid up front, signed contracts and a settlement agreed for the divorce at the end. He wanted an educated attractive Englishwoman and I stepped forward. I almost told his lawyers that he could have two of us for the price of one!'

Alissa wasn't amused by that rather tasteless joke. 'So, let me get this straight—you decided you were willing to marry this man just for the cash?'

'For Mum!' Alexa contradicted loudly. 'I was only *ever* willing to do it for her sake.'

Alissa sat there tautly and thought about this explanation. Everything she herself had done of late, from resigning from her comfortable librarian's job in London to coming home to help out as best she could, had also been done for her mother's sake. Both young women adored their parent, who was currently stressed out of her mind and desperately depressed, a mere shadow of the cheerful and energetic woman she had once been.

A kinder and more loving and supportive parent or wife than Jenny Bartlett would be hard to find. Unfortunately, over the past two years, the twins' once close and contented family circle had been cruelly smashed by a series of disasters. The death of their brother, Stephen, and of Alexa's boyfriend, Peter, in a car crash one wintry evening had only been the first calamity to strike them. That storm had barely been weathered before their father's cancer was diagnosed. Long months of anxiety and debilitating medical treatment had followed. Throughout all those events their mother had been the strongest of them all, refusing to allow her family to sink into despair. She could never have guessed then that, within months of his recovery from cancer, her husband of thirty years would desert her for a much younger woman and then claim half of their home and business to finance his new lifestyle. Watching those awful proceedings unfold from the sidelines, Alissa had felt her heart break alongside her mother's.

Alissa had learned a new insecurity when she had finally realised that she could not even trust her father to be the honest and decent man she had always believed he was. Although he was an accountant on a good salary, he was pursuing his wife for a share of the home that had originally belonged to *her* parents and of the small business that she had set up and ran entirely on her own. Money and the lust for more of it, Alissa thought fearfully, could turn people into strangers and make them do inexcusable things. Now it seemed to her that Alexa had got caught up in the same dangerous toils.

'Pay the money back,' Alissa urged tightly. 'You can't marry some foreigner you don't even know for money.'

'Well, I can't marry him *now*, can I? I mean, I'm carrying Harry's baby!' Alexa pointed out flatly. 'And Harry wants us to get married in the next couple of weeks.'

Alissa nodded, unsurprised by that sudden announcement. Alissa always did everything at supersonic speed. That she had fallen in love and fallen pregnant within months and was racing equally fast into marriage was the norm for her. She had never learnt patience and if common sense threatened to come between her and her goals she would ignore it.

'*You* must go ahead and marry the Russian in my place,' Alexa continued, 'or I'll be forced to consider an abortion…'

Shattered by that announcement, Alissa pushed her chair noisily back and leapt upright. 'What on earth are you talking about? *Me* marry this weird guy? An *abortion?* Is that what you want?'

A petulant expression traversed Alexa's face. 'No, of course it's not what I want, Allie, but what choice do I have? I signed a legal binding contract and I accepted a huge amount of money on the strength of it. Most of the money has been spent so I can't give it back. So where does that leave me?'

Alissa was once again aghast at that admission. '*Spent?*'

'Mostly on Mum. Okay, so I bought the car and a few other little things. At the time I thought that with the sacrifice I was making in agreeing to marry the guy, I had the right to spoil myself a bit. After all, it was me, not you, riding to Mum's rescue!' her twin vented, treating her sister to a scornful appraisal. 'I mean, here you are, acting all shocked at what I've done. But what have *you* done, but sit here wringing your hands and checking bank statements? It took me to take action, so don't you dare look down on me for being willing to marry a stranger for money. Money and lots of it is the only real cure for the problems here!'

The louder Alexa's angry voice got, the paler Alissa became and she sat down heavily again. 'I'm not looking down on you in any way. You're right. You have pulled off something that I couldn't have and, yes, we are desperate for money—'

Her sister clasped her hand in a fierce plea for understanding. 'Don't I deserve to be happy?'

'I've never doubted it.'

'But I never thought I'd be happy again after Peter died. I thought my life was over, that I might as well have died in that car with him and Stephen,' Alexa confided in a pained tone. 'But now I've met Harry and everything's different. I love him and I want to marry him and have my baby. I've got my life back again and I want to enjoy it.'

Touched to the bone by that emotive speech, Alissa clasped both her hands round her sister's in a warm gesture of understanding. 'Of course you do…of course you do…'

'But Harry won't want anything more to do with me if he finds out what I signed up for—it will *destroy* us!' Alexa sobbed, swerving from furious defensiveness and drama to a noisy bout of self-pitying tears. 'He would never understand what I've done or forgive me for being so mercenary. He's a very straightforward, honest man.'

All of a sudden, Alissa was feeling as though she was on old familiar ground. When they were children, Alexa had often got into tight corners and Alissa had usually got her out of them. More than once Alissa had shouldered the blame for Alexa's wrongdoing, as even then she had dimly grasped that she might be the less adventurous twin but she *was* the stronger and the least likely of the two to break down when life became difficult. Alexa might be more daring, but she was also surprisingly fragile and could never cope once she made a mess of things.

'Surely Harry doesn't have to know about all this?' Alissa said, even though she felt guilty for suggesting that Alexa keep secrets from her future husband.

'Listen, Allie,' Alexa breathed. 'If I don't show up and marry the Russian, I'll have to repay the money and I can't. Do you honestly think a guy like Sergei Antonovich is going to let me get away with defrauding him of that amount of cash?'

'Sergei Antonovich? The Russian billionaire?' Alissa queried in consternation. 'He's the guy who wants to hire a wife? For goodness' sake, he's always knee-deep in supermodels and actresses. Why would he have to *pay* a woman he doesn't know to marry him?'

'Because a long time ago he was married and it didn't work out. This time around he wants a marriage of convenience on a strict business basis. I don't know any more than that,' Alexa replied, her eyes swerving abruptly from her sister's questioning gaze to rest fixedly on the table instead, her whole face taut and shuttered. 'That was what the lawyer told me and he said I didn't need to know any more and that it was just a job; maybe a little different from other jobs, but a job nonetheless.'

'A job,' Alissa repeated, widening her expressive eyes in emphatic disagreement.

'If you marry Antonovich instead, I'll be able to go ahead and marry Harry, we'll keep the money and Mum's life will go back to normal. You know, the Russian hasn't met me yet, so he won't know we've switched and he's never going to guess that you're not the woman who was selected—'

'It doesn't matter…it's crazy and I couldn't do it,' Alissa framed unevenly, feeling the weight of the pressure her twin was heaping on her shoulders and firmly resisting it.

'I applied in your name,' her sister reminded her. 'It's you the lawyers will come after if you don't follow through on that contract.'

Alissa, usually slow to lose her temper, was finally getting angry. 'I don't care what you did—*I* didn't sign any contract!'

'Well, you might as well have done because I forged your signature,' Alexa informed her wryly. 'I'm sorry, but we're both involved in this up to our throats. Short of a lottery win, we can't return the money and why would you want to anyway? We've no other way of saving this house for Mum. At the moment, it's impossible to get a loan—'

'But Mum couldn't have afforded to pay it back anyway. And now there's not even anything left to sell,' Alissa acknowledged.

The few valuable pieces of furniture and jewellery that had been in the family had already been sold to shore up her mother's finances. The cottage had long been mortgaged up to the hilt when Jenny had borrowed against the property to buy premises in the village and open up a coffee and craft shop there. Although the cottage was currently for sale, there had been few viewers and little interest shown; times were hard and the property was definitely in need of modernisation.

In the uncomfortable silence that stretched, Alissa stood up. 'It's raining—I promised I'd pick Mum up if it was wet.'

Alissa climbed into the elderly hatchback car that belonged to her mother and drove off. As she pulled into a parking space outside the shop, she saw a curvaceous brunette emerging and unfurling a bright yellow plastic umbrella. She wore a skirt short enough to shock a burlesque dancer. At the sight of her, loud alarm bells rang with Alissa because the woman was her father's girlfriend, Maggie Lines. As Maggie sped on down the street Alissa scrambled out of the car in haste and knocked on the shop door when she found it locked.

'What was that woman doing in here?' she demanded of the small blonde woman who let her in.

Her mother's eyes were reddened and overbright, her level of stress palpable in her fearful expression and trembling hands. 'She came to talk to me. She said she didn't like to come to the house and at least she waited for closing time—'

Alissa was rigid with outrage on her gentle mother's behalf. She felt that it was bad enough that her father had had an affair but it was unspeakably cruel that he should allow his partner in crime to harass the wife he had deserted. 'You don't need to talk to Maggie. She's Dad's business, not yours, and she should keep her nose out of what doesn't concern her!'

'She says that fighting it out between the lawyers is only increasing our legal bills,' Jenny muttered tautly.

'What did she want?' Alissa prompted, carefully removing the dishcloth that her mother was twisting between her nervous hands.

'Money. What she said is your father's due,' the older woman explained in a mortified undertone. 'And although I didn't like hearing it, what she said was right. It *is* the law that he has to get his share of everything, but there's not a lot I can do when we haven't even had an offer for the house, is there?'

'She shouldn't have come here. You shouldn't have to speak to her.'

'She's a very determined young woman but I'm not scared of her, Alissa. And you shouldn't be getting involved in all this. Your father may well marry Maggie and start a second family with her. It happens all the time, so it would be wiser if you didn't take sides right now.'

Her troubled eyes glistening with tears, Alissa gripped the older woman's hands tightly in hers. 'I love you so much, Mum. I hate to see you being hurt like this.'

Jenny Bartlett attempted a reassuring smile. 'In time I'll get over it, "move on" as Maggie likes to say. But right now it's all too fresh. I *still* love him, Alissa,' she muttered guiltily. 'That's the worst thing about all this. I can't seem to switch off my feelings.'

Alissa wrapped her arms protectively round her slight mother. Her own heart felt as if it were breaking inside her as a swell of memories from happier times engulfed her. It was not right that the mother who had loved and supported her all her life should lose her home and business as well, for it would leave the older woman with absolutely nothing to survive on. 'Alexa's home, Mum, and she's got good news: she's met a man and it's serious—'

The older woman turned startled eyes on her daughter. 'Has she…*really?*'

'Yes, and Alexa and I have sorted out something on the money front too,' Alissa heard herself say with deliberate vagueness. 'You may not have to sell the house after all.'

'That's not possible,' Jenny exclaimed.

'Miracles do happen,' Alissa commented, thinking

up fantastic stories of special financial arrangements that could be made and secured on her and her twin's earning power.

And she was stunned by her own audacity. She was the sensible twin, the one who was never impulsive and didn't take risks. But family came first and she was desperate to help and bring the ghastly divorce settlement to a dignified conclusion for her mother's sake. She watched the older woman lock up. So, did that mean she was willing to marry Sergei Antonovich? Or had she just been guilty of offering her mother false hope? During the short drive home Alissa tussled mentally with herself.

A few minutes after she walked through the front door, however, Alexa helped her to make a final decision. 'I got a call from the Russian's lawyer while you were out,' her twin whispered in Alissa's ear while Alissa was busy preparing supper. 'Sergei Antonovich has decided to meet me before the wedding. You have to decide whether you're going to help Mum or not!'

Put on the spot, Alissa thought first about the baby that her twin was carrying and doubted Alexa's readiness to continue that pregnancy if her relationship with the father ran into trouble. In comparison Alissa had no relationship that such a marriage could interfere with.

A long time ago, she had suffered considerable heartache when she'd secretly fallen for Alexa's boyfriend, Peter. Since then she had made occasional forays onto the dating scene, only to retreat when she met up with the impatient sexual expectations of the modern male. Those who had failed to press her panic buttons on that score had signally failed to impress her on any other level. Unlike Alexa, who scalp-hunted with almost masculine enthusiasm, Alissa preferred quality over quantity and was more often alone than involved in a relationship.

Indeed her family meant much more to Alissa than anything else in her life. Having had to stand by powerless while that same family had all but disintegrated had tortured her. But now Alexa had put the power to alter that situation into Alissa's hands. Did she have the strength to go against her every principle and make a mockery of marriage by using it as a means of making money? Did the fact that she had no plans to profit personally make it any less of a sin? And now that she had that option, could she honestly turn her back on the only chance she was ever likely to get to settle most of her mother's problems?

On the other hand, Alissa reasoned, money would not bring her father home or cure her mother's pain, but it would certainly help the older woman to adjust to her altered future if it allowed her to remain in her childhood home and retain her business. On that optimistic thought, Alissa squashed the doubts bubbling up frantically to the surface of her mind. Pretending to be some man's wife would be a challenge, but the return of some semblance of normality to her mother's life would be worth it. On reaching that conclusion, Alissa came to a swift decision and gave Alexa the answer she most wanted to hear…

CHAPTER TWO

FROWNING, Sergei surveyed the studio photo for at least the tenth time that morning. Taken feature by feature, Alissa Bartlett was very attractive but regrettably she didn't *do* anything for him.

Sergei, who had never suffered from indecision, was fighting a galloping attack of cold feet. Having noted that his lawyers hadn't done much research into his bride-to-be's background, he had already resolved to have that omission rectified before he went any further. But, if he was honest, his main objection to her was a good deal more basic: in a nutshell, the skinny blonde turned him off big time.

He had read the transcripts of her interviews and studied her psychological profile and, the more he found out about her, the less he wanted to marry her, even temporarily. The trouble was that she *did* tick all the boxes he had demanded be ticked. In that respect, his staff had done an excellent job. He could not deny that she was attractive, educated, sophisticated and elegant. But then he had failed to lay down the right criteria for the role. He had thought too much about what was on the outside and not enough about what was on the inside, for it was plain Alissa was also selfish, extremely vain, rather stupid in spite of that education and cold as ice in the emotional department.

However, since when had he wanted emotion involved in a relationship with a woman? Sergei asked himself with derision. But then, never before had he been confronted in advance by so many unpalatable facts about a woman's character. Furthermore, Yelena was nobody's fool and was almost certain to spot the ugly truth below the pretty surface show of such a wife. That was why Sergei had decided that he *had* to meet his chosen bride in the flesh rather than risking compounding his mistake by marrying her sight unseen in a week's time. He didn't want to leave anything to chance. He could always cancel the contract if she didn't come up to scratch in the flesh. He cursed under his breath, wondering if all his carefully laid plans were about to come to nothing...

'This just isn't me,' Alissa sighed, studying her reflection in the mirror with critical and uneasy eyes.

'You're not supposed to be you, you're supposed to be *me*—at least to look at!' Alexa argued vehemently. 'And you can't show up in some cut-price dreary outfit when I was supposed to choose a new wardrobe in time for the wedding and given the money to do it. I'm going to have to give you almost all my clothes to go through with this masquerade.'

Recognising the resentful note in her twin's voice, Alissa breathed, 'I don't want your clothes because they're not my style '

'You don't *have* a style,' her more fashionable sister

retorted tartly. 'You wear cheap comfy clothes and that's not what a rich man expects. If you're going to carry this pretence off, you have to get the image right.'

'If you added a set of wings I'd look just like a fairy off a Christmas tree!' Alissa exclaimed in mortification, twirling so that the short skirt of the black dress flew out and exposed the cerise-pink layers of net edged with lace beneath. The net was scratchy and uncomfortable and the towering pink peep-toe shoes she also wore forced her to walk in little mincing steps. Plus, she was a good deal curvier than her sister and her breasts were straining against the snug fit of the bodice. 'This dress is too small for me!'

'It's fine. I have a much slimmer figure. You can't expect the dress to look anything like as good on you as it does on me. Try to remember that it's not cool to stuff yourself if there's food around,' Alexa reprimanded her. 'You're welcome to my clothes. After all I am pregnant and they won't fit me much longer. Make sure you don't lose that coat by leaving it down somewhere. There are thieves everywhere.'

A towering man, who was as tall as he was broad, came to the door of Alexa's apartment to announce that a car was waiting downstairs for Alissa. Alexa was careful to stay out of sight. He had a heavy accent and minimal English at his disposal, so Alissa's initial chatty efforts to find out what his name was, how long he had worked for his employer and where she was going fell on stony ground. During the journey, however, he turned in the front passenger seat, eased open the partition and pointed carefully to himself. 'Borya,' he told her, having worked out what she wanted to know.

'Alissa,' she responded cheerfully, striving not to surrender to the nervous chill steadily spreading through her.

The vehicle came to a halt outside a nightclub where a sizeable gathering of stylish people were already queuing for entry. A protective presence by her side, Borya swept her in past the doormen. Mindful of her twin's strictures about the coat she wore, Alissa came to a halt at the cloakroom check and removed the garment, determined to take no risks with it. Borya broke into a voluble speech but she was none the wiser as to what he was telling her and she passed over the coat.

'Are you feeling all right?' she asked the attendant, who was coughing into a handkerchief and shivering in the corner behind the counter.

'I've got a rotten cold and it's freezing in here,' the girl spluttered miserably and Alissa felt desperately sorry for her; while she had been a student she had often worked in low-paid part-time jobs to make ends meet.

Surrounded by his aides and his entire security team, Sergei was in a private room watching football on a giant wall television plasma screen. But the instant his bride-to-be walked through the door backed by Borya, he shook himself by totally forgetting the game. Indeed unfamiliar words like exquisite and dazzling briefly shone a glow of inspiration over Sergei's more usually prosaic thoughts. He was initially off-balanced by the reality that Alissa did not seem to bear much resemblance to her photo. In the flesh she was so much more than merely attractive. In fact she was incredibly feminine with a beautiful heart-shaped face, delicate features and aquamarine eyes as blue-green and mysterious as the sea. Long golden blonde hair tumbled halfway down her back. She was also tiny, the dress drawing attention to her minuscule waist and the pouting upward swell of the surprisingly full curves above it. His attention rested on her lush Cupid's bow mouth and the firm rounded globes of her breasts. The tightness at his groin shifted into the heaviness of solid arousal and his galloping attack of cold feet just vanished there and then. Somehow the photo had lied: she was gorgeous and very beddable.

When Alissa saw the big dark male sprawled on the sofa, she fell still and had to be urged forward. In slow motion he came fluidly upright, well over six feet of long, lean, powerfully built masculinity unfolding before her intimidated gaze. He was a stunningly handsome guy. Black hair was brushed back from his lean bronzed face, which was dissected by the arrogant blade of his nose and complemented by high carved cheekbones and an aggressive jaw line. Her ability to swallow and breathe was arrested while she stood there staring. He was blatantly male in an age when that primal attribute was becoming more and more rare. Glittering, very dark eyes flared down into hers and her heart succumbed to a nervous bounce behind her ribcage.

'Come and sit down,' Sergei murmured, his accent purring over syllables that took more concentration than usual to pronounce. 'I'm watching my club play. Do you follow football?'

'No, not at all,' Alissa admitted, scanning his appearance. He wore a black striped designer shirt, the sleeves of which he had pushed up his arms, and well-cut black trousers. The jacket of his business suit lay in a heap and his silk tie was in the process of falling off the coffee table onto the floor. She could tell at a glance that he was untidy and that he most probably had a low tolerance threshold for any kind of restriction. His tightly leashed energy hummed in the air like a building storm while he automatically took up a strong stance of authority.

Sergei, who was accustomed to women who raved about football for his benefit, was stunned by that careless response. 'You don't like football?' he repeated, giving her another chance to reconsider and ingratiate herself.

'I've never thought about it one way or the other. I wasn't one of the girls who wanted to play it at school anyway,' Alissa confided as she lifted his jacket, folded it and set it neatly aside so that she could sit down. The tie on the floor irritated her but she struggled not to pick it up. After all, she wasn't his maid. 'I wasn't the sporty type.'

She was small-boned and fragile and the idea of her on a football pitch struck him as ludicrous. He snapped imperious fingers like a potentate presiding over a court and the waiter hovering by the door hurried over to take his order for pink vodka. A tall bottle arrived and drinks were poured. Alissa accepted a glass and wished she were able to ask some of the dozen questions brimming on her lips, but she could not afford to expose her ignorance and risk blowing her cover. Trying not to wince at the strong taste of the drink, she sipped.

'You don't like vodka either?' Sergei quipped, wondering why she was so uptight, sitting perched on the very edge of the sofa and maintaining a careful distance from him.

At that comment, which strongly suggested that she was not meeting his expectations, Alissa deemed it wisest to tip her head back and down what remained in the glass in one go. It was like swallowing flames and she thought her burning throat would never be the same again. Another bottle arrived with a fresh pair of glasses.

'Try this one and see if it is more to your taste—it's made in Scotland,' Sergei informed her lazily.

'I'm okay—I don't drink an awful lot.' Alissa continued to clutch her empty glass to make it easier to avoid the offer of another.

'You should enjoy alcohol while you still can,' he told her.

Alissa wondered what on earth she was supposed to make of that piece of advice. What did he mean? That if she signed on the dotted line as his wife she would no longer be allowed to drink? The sudden outcry from the men in the room accompanied by a full-throated roar from the spectators of the game on the television stole her attention.

'Oh, someone's scored, have they?' she commented brightly, forgetting that odd remark of his in her eagerness to make conversation. Nobody needed to tell her that her sister, Alexa, would not have been sitting there by his side as quiet as a little mouse. 'How exciting…'

'Alissa,' Sergei said gently, 'it was the other team, *not* mine, which scored.'

Colour flamed in her cheeks. 'Oh, dear…'

Sergei closed long fingers round the small hand curling into the sofa by her side and used that connection to propel her across the space separating them.

'What are you doing?' Alissa gasped, instant panic flooding through her.

Unperturbed, Sergei drew her right up to him and brushed the golden hair back from her cheeks with confident fingers. All big eyes and fluctuating colour, she was breathing rapidly. It was not the flirtatious or amused reaction he expected to receive from an experienced woman and he was intrigued. 'What do you think?' he mocked.

She collided with dark eyes flaring lustrous gold and a tight clenching sensation in her pelvis made her shift uncomfortably in her seat. She gazed up at him, terrified that any attempt to go into retreat or call a halt would have the same provocative effect on his intrinsically dominant nature as a gauntlet thrown down in challenge. As her nipples tightened into stinging prominence she sucked in a ragged breath and pressed her thighs tensely together. She knew what was happening to her and she didn't like it at all. Her body was attracted to him, not her brain, she told herself angrily. Her brain had nothing to do with the desire that was assailing her in a seductive tide.

'You're very sexy,' Sergei husked, a long finger tracing the voluptuous raspberry-tinted curve of her lower lip while his hungry body reacted with almost painful enthusiasm to the sensual pull of her fragrant body so close to his. 'Come home with me tonight. Why should we wait?'

Her aquamarine eyes flew even wider and she lowered her lashes hurriedly in self-defence. They had only met a few minutes ago and he actually thought she would be willing to sleep with him tonight? He *expected* her to sleep with him? He could only be asking why they should wait for the wedding. If Alexa had been sitting beside her at that moment, Alissa would definitely have strangled her twin. Exactly what kind of an arrangement had Alexa signed up for with this man? And how could Alissa challenge his assumptions without revealing her ignorance and running the risk of being unveiled as an impostor?

The atmosphere vibrated like a tautly strung musical instrument. In the midst of the frantic thoughts racing inside Alissa's head, Sergei tugged her to him and brought his wide shapely mouth crashing hungrily down on hers. It was sweeter than sweet in intensity and hotter than flames. Fireworks of response were set off like a chain reaction of energy snaking through her slender body. She had never before got a charge like that from a kiss and the power of it shocked her. He parted her lips with his tongue and delved sensually deep in the moist interior of her mouth and she shuddered with the wicked, wanton pleasure of it. The smouldering prickle of heat between her thighs raised her temperature even more. Her fingers were lodged in the luxuriant thickness of his black hair, but she craved much closer contact than she already had. She wanted to press herself fully against his lean, hard body.

'Enough, *milaya moya*.' Sergei set her back from him with urgent hands while he scanned her hectically flushed face and the lack of focus in her eyes with satisfaction. She was seriously hot and passionate. He liked a woman who could forget herself so totally in his arms. He was already picturing that tiny lush body splayed across his bed, and the wedding he had begun to dread finally acquired a strong source of appeal. Getting his wife pregnant did, at the very least, promise to be a highly entertaining pursuit.

Disorientated, Alissa blinked, not quite ready to accept that she could have let him kiss her breathless while making no attempt to end their embrace. She was in a state of complete bewilderment.

'The game,' Sergei murmured succinctly as if it was the only thing in the world that mattered at that moment.

Alissa almost lifted one of the bottles off the table and brained him with it. He was talking about football! The football was more important than she was? Her soft swollen mouth snapping shut like a steel strap, Alissa murmured sweetly, 'I like a man who has his priorities in the right place.'

Sergei would have suspected sarcasm if it were not for the fact that women were invariably too busy trying to impress him to snipe at him. He turned his attention back to the television screen. 'I'll take you down to the nightclub when the game is over.'

The colour in her cheeks high, Alissa stared at the television screen and childishly hoped his team would lose. She had let him kiss her in front of a room full of men. She had completely forgotten where she was, who she was with and who she was supposed to be pretending to be. How could she have behaved like that with a man she barely knew? And would he just have pushed Alexa away and gone back to watching his stupid game? Why, all of a sudden, was she thinking like a jealous insecure teenager? Wouldn't she be better engaged wondering *why* Sergei Antonovich had suggested she spend the night with him? Most jobs, even unusual ones, were conducted in a more professional and considerably less intimate manner.

Sergei could feel her boredom and it irritated him. It was bad enough that his team was losing. Indeed, in spite of the millions he had poured into his football club, it was a bloodbath on that pitch! He began to explain the game to her, astonished by a level of ignorance that ensured that she even had to ask the meaning of the simplest of terms. No, she definitely wasn't sporty and she had clearly made no effort to discover his interests and prepare for them so that she could be a good companion. He was annoyed that she had been so lazy. No Russian woman would have made such a cardinal error when it came to pleasing a man. On the other hand he was convinced she would please him very much in bed and he was strong enough to mould her like wax into what he wanted in every other field.

Alissa accompanied him into the lift. 'This place is enormous.'

'I extended it to provide VIP rooms. It's very popular. The staff are trained to deliver the service that Russians expect,' Sergei advanced, taking advantage of the mirrored walls to study her from all angles and finding no view that disappointed him. There was no denying that she was little, but in all the right womanly places she was deliciously rounded, which compensated for her lack of height.

'You own this club?' Alissa said in surprise.

'Yes. There wasn't a club in London able to offer the level of facilities that I expect.'

She had never met a man of such blazing assurance. She sensed that that confidence defined him. He expected the very best and refused to accept less, which was why he had bought his own nightclub and personalised it to suit his needs. So demanding and confident a male must have found an unsuccessful first marriage intolerable. Did that explain why he had chosen to opt for a businesslike approach for his second marital venture? It was unlikely, Alissa decided when she recalled the salient fact that this proposed marriage was only to last a couple of years at most. Normal marriages didn't take off with the divorce date already in place. So, why was he bothering to get married?

'You're very quiet,' Sergei commented as the lift doors purred open, letting in a flood of voices and pounding music.

From that point, there was no further opportunity for speech. Men she recognised now from his security team were standing by an empty table, keeping it reserved for their employer. But no sooner had Sergei stepped onto the dance floor to approach that table than the front-runners in a surge of excited women engulfed him. Alissa had never seen anything like it. She was nudged back by the tide, pushed aside, left standing while various women giggled, reached out to try and touch him and performed dance steps as though they were auditioning for Sergei's benefit. It was no wonder that he exuded the air of a man accustomed to being the centre of attention for he very definitely was, just as there was no doubt that he could have walked away from his admirers had he so desired.

Alissa lifted her head high and left him to it, taking a seat behind the table where Borya was stationed. With two beautiful women on either side of him and visibly hanging on his every word, Sergei appeared to be in his element. And he *was*, Alissa acknowledged, because Sergei Antonovich was a notorious womaniser or, depending on one's outlook, a famous connoisseur of her sex. Over the years he had appeared in a lot of tabloid

pictures, always with a different gorgeous woman cling-
ing to him as he emerged from nightclubs, stood on yacht
decks or posed in front of the impressive Antonovich
building that housed his business empire in London.
Although he was not known for fidelity or for the lon-
gevity of his affairs, a long list of fabulous beauties had
still accepted him on those demeaning terms.

Sergei looked around for Alissa and could barely
credit that she had simply walked off and sat down. In
all his life a woman had never treated him to such a display of indifference and it infuriated him. They were
getting married in a week! He had just organised the
publicity release on that score and there was his bride
ignoring him, demonstrating her inability to meet the
demands of the role she had been hired to play. No normal woman in love with a man would leave him with a
bevy of willing and seductive beauties milling around
him.

Stony-faced and unimpressed, Alissa sipped vodka
through compressed lips while Sergei danced and flirted
with the collection of truly shameless and determined
women. There was the fatal flaw in all that wealth,
power and potent male beauty, Alissa reflected with
simmering scorn. Sergei Antonovich had no manners
and not the smallest idea of how to behave in public with
the woman he was planning to marry. That was undoubtedly why he had to *pay* a woman to take on the
job. No woman with any pride or dignity would tolerate
such treatment, not to mention the arrogant assumption
that she would be happy to watch a bunch of football-
ers chasing a stupid ball round a muddy pitch at their
very first meeting. If it had been a real date, Alissa

would already have labelled him a loser and headed for home. Now she was wondering how long she was obligated to sit in public letting him make a fool of her while he dallied with the deferential type of oversexed woman he clearly preferred.

Alissa's fingertips began to drum a little tattoo on the table top while she watched Sergei and she decided that she was leaving within the next ten minutes. She was irritated when someone blocked her view and she glanced up in surprise as a handsome blond man in a suit spoke to her in spite of Borya's attempts to head him off. He was asking her to dance. Well, why not? Why should she sit bored, like a prisoner at her guarded table? Alissa rose from her seat, slid out from behind the table and off she went.

Sergei, who had little experience of women who fought back on his own level, was astounded to be forced to witness the reality that his future wife could dance in a very suggestive manner with another man. Dark eyes colder than a Siberian winter, he watched Alissa wriggle her curvaceous hips and turn, short skirt flying up to reveal the pink lace-edged net and a pair of very shapely, slender legs. He strode across the floor and, with an aggressive jerk of his head at her partner, he cut in, lifting his hands to rest them on her slight shoulders.

'What the hell do you think you're playing at?' he demanded rawly in the interval when the music paused before coming back again on an even more deafening beat.

Alissa was stunned by the level of aggression in his behaviour and was not at all surprised that the man she had been dancing with beat a safe sensible retreat, for she suspected that Sergei was quite capable of getting physical. In an abrupt movement that took him by surprise she shrugged off his hands and stalked off the floor. She was going home and she didn't care how he felt about it. She wasn't prepared to spend one more minute in a domineering brute's company!

Sergei's anger was laced with outrage and a profound and lingering sense of disbelief because her defiant refusal to conform to his expectations was the direct opposite of the treatment he was used to receiving from a woman. He strode off in her wake, snatching out his cell phone to answer it when it buzzed. It was the owner of the firm he used to do background screening calling to tell him that it would take much more time than was available before the wedding to do the usual full in-depth check on Alissa. Sergei studied the tiny stalking figure ahead of him, the swirl of her short skirt, the defiant angle of her little shoulders, and told his caller to forget about the check altogether. Just then he knew that, whatever happened, he intended to have her in his bed and to hell with the risk!

Alissa stopped at the coat-check facility, for she had no intention of drawing down Alexa's ire by abandoning her sister's much-prized coat.

'What do you think you're doing?' Sergei growled from several feet away.

'I'm going home. I don't date Neanderthal men and the only place you belong is a cave!' Alissa sizzled back at him without hesitation.

'You're not on a date,' Sergei reminded her with biting cool, reluctantly amused by the 'Neanderthal man' crack, but also offended even though nothing would have made him betray that crucial fact.

In an impatient movement he stepped forward and addressed the coat check attendant. 'Get a move on,' he urged. 'We are in a hurry.'

'Don't be so rude!' Alissa launched at him. 'She's not feeling well. She doesn't need you barking orders at her like she's in the army.'

All amusement evaporating, Sergei drew in a long slow breath and suppressed his volcanic temper with some difficulty. Borya and his men were already stationed by the exit, transfixed by the scene being enacted fifteen feet from them. What sort of a woman dared to tell him how to behave? Criticised him? Threatened to walk out on him? He flicked a glance at the shocked coat-check girl, who was coughing noisily into a hanky and simultaneously trying to shrink into the back of her cubbyhole. What sort of a woman cared about the health or the feelings of a menial employee? A kinder woman than the more selfish type he usually spent his time with, he conceded grudgingly. Her altruistic concern reminded him of Yelena, who had long been the first port of call when neighbours fell sick or needed someone to mind their children. Here was a woman who might, with his guidance, turn into exactly the kind of wife he wanted to produce for his grandmother's inspection.

Alissa watched Sergei settle a high denomination banknote down on the counter in a silent apology. Oh, how she wished the girl would fling it back in his handsome teeth and demand the words instead, but of course she didn't. In obvious awe of him, she stammered heartfelt thanks and pocketed the money at a speed that shook Alissa. He took the coat and extended it with a flourish for Alissa.

She dug her arms into it and froze as his lean warm hands lifted her hair from her nape where it had caught beneath the collar. The gentle brush of his fingertips against her skin burned through her sensitised body like a match flame lighting dry crackling straw. That fast she remembered the raw, demanding sensuality and pressure of his mouth and her body reacted to the memory with an instantaneous rush of heat and moisture between her thighs. Unbearably aware of her body's wanton vulnerability, she froze.

Sergei eased her back against his big powerful frame and ran lean, sure hands down her sleeves to lift and enclose her hands in the warm, firm grip of his. Unable to maintain her rigid stance and wildly aware of his proximity, she trembled.

'The press are waiting outside and you are about to enjoy your fifteen minutes of fame,' he murmured lazily, the rich dark tone of his deep voice feathering like a caress along her spine. 'It's time to start acting and look happy to be with me.'

Alissa was bemused by that information. The press? She felt out of her depth and knew that, most ironically, her sister would have loved such a moment in the public eye. 'So I can't slap you, then?'

Sergei vented a roughened masculine laugh that made her more than ever conscious of his sexual pulling power. 'No.'

'Or sulk?'

'I wouldn't put up with it, *milaya moya*. Just like I won't stand another man laying a single finger on any part of you while you're supposed to be mine,' he added with a studious casualness that somehow made what he was

saying all the more riveting. 'With me there are boundaries and you *must* respect them. Do I need to say any
more?'

Picking up on the intimidating chill in his intonation,
Alissa almost shivered, but she was bone-deep resistant
to domination of any kind. 'Were you born a bully? Or
do you find you have to work at it?'

Sergei was utterly poleaxed by that impudent comeback. Black brows descending over grim dark eyes, he
stared down at the shining blonde head that barely
reached the centre of his chest, his long brown fingers
still instinctively engaged in stroking the fine-boned
fragility of her wrists. She was the size of a doll and she
was fighting him every step of the way. He could not
even begin to credit her bravado.

'Your silence tells me that it comes naturally to you,'
Alissa answered for herself and even she was wondering why she was going out on a limb to hit back at him.
Was it the effect of the vodka? Or his behaviour with
female admirers, which had paraded his total lack of
interest in her feelings? Or the ghastly embarrassing
truth that she found him stupendously attractive in spite
of his overpoweringly masculine ways?

Sergei bent to clamp his hands to her waist and then
he lifted her bodily around to face him. 'By the time I'm
finished with you, you will *love* football—'

Seriously vexed at being lifted off her feet and treated
like a child, Alissa focused on him with blazing aquamarine eyes. 'Dream on!'

'And once you get used to me you'll be jealous and
clingy and adoring just like all the other women I've
ever known,' Sergei completed with raw conviction.

In the hold of his hands, her fingers balled into furious fists. 'I don't think you can ever have met a woman like me before.'

His brilliant dark eyes flamed golden as the heart of a fire and he looked dangerous, his lean, dark, handsome face taut. '*Stoy*…stop!' he spelt out with critical cool. 'Have you forgotten why you are here with me?'

Her lashes lowered and she was suddenly still and fighting to get a grip on her angry discomfiture. His reminder had been timely: she *had* forgotten. He had hired Alexa to carry out a role and so far Alissa had annoyed him, disagreed with him and argued with him. She breathed in slow and deep to calm herself.

'That is better,' Sergei pronounced and he lowered his arrogant dark head and pressed his lips gently to her lush pink mouth.

And for the merest fraction of a second she resisted the urge to part her lips before the throb of the blood in her veins and the acceleration of her heartbeat combined to vanquish her defences. Suddenly, without even being aware of the prompting, she tipped her head back and let him taste her again, glorying in the shimmering, prickling mist of coming-alive sensation surging through her again. The flick of his tongue against the tender roof of her mouth made her shiver and press forward, instinctively wanting more.

'Now we will go outside,' Sergei breathed, lifting his handsome dark head and tugging her beneath one arm.

The bank of cameras and shouted questions that greeted their appearance made her shrink back against the arm locked to her slender spine. Aquamarine eyes huge, she contrived an uncertain smile while his bodyguards fanned out around them to prevent anyone from getting too close. She didn't breathe again until she was safe inside the limousine and invisible behind the tinted windows. She was in a daze, unable to credit that she had let him kiss her again and that, in truth, she could hardly wait for a repetition. It was as if one little taste of him had created a terrifying craving she could not suppress.

'You didn't enjoy the attention,' Sergei remarked, his questioning gaze locked to her pale face. 'It frightened you—why?'

'I suppose I'm rather a private sort of person.'

'That is not the impression you gave in your interviews.'

Alissa had felt safe from detection in his presence because he had never met her sister. But evidently her sister's interviews had been recorded in some way and he was aware of the content and had formed advance opinions about her personality on that basis. Suddenly she was very tense. 'Everyone puts their best foot forward in an interview situation.'

Sergei made no comment but he noticed her evasiveness and wondered what lay behind it. 'You have to learn to relax with me. In less than a week we're flying to Russia for our wedding.'

'Russia,' Alissa echoed weakly, plunging into even deeper consternation at the concept while she asked herself if she could possibly go through with the role her twin had agreed to play.

'This is for you.' Sergei handed her a parcel. 'We'll be able to keep in touch now. I've been too distant from this process, *milaya moya*.'

It was Alexa who took the trouble to rip the wrapping

off the parcel twenty minutes later. Goggle-eyed, she studied the mobile phone she had extracted and she let out a sudden whoop. 'Oh, wow, I can't believe it. He's given you only one of the most expensive phones in the world! See those…' She extended the phone to her sister. 'Those are real diamonds.'

'Are they?' Alissa was unable to share her excitement for, while she could admire the glitter of the diamonds, she could not see the point of such decoration on a mobile phone. Indeed that level of adornment struck her as an embarrassingly pretentious display of wealth.

'This is worth thousands and thousands of pounds and I'm more entitled to it than you are!' Alexa suddenly concluded, shooting Alissa a resentful glance. 'I'm the one who won this job and now you're getting all the stuff that should have been mine—'

Alissa was less interested in the phone than in the wedding on the horizon. 'Why do you think Sergei Antonovich wants a wife in the first place? Aren't you curious?'

Alexa's face shuttered and she pursed her lips. 'Not really. As long as it's nothing illegal, I couldn't care less why. Maybe it'll give him some sort of tax or business or inheritance advantage, or perhaps he wants a wife to give him a breathing space from all the pushy women who target him.'

'Sergei certainly didn't strike me as the marrying type,' Alissa confided. 'He also asked me to spend the night with him—'

Eyes rounding in shock, Alexa studied her twin with a dropped jaw. 'He *did*? He found you that attractive? I bet you thought all your Christmases had come at once. Why did you leave him to come back here, for goodness' sake?'

Her face hot in receipt of that revealing response, Alissa murmured, 'The point is…why did he ask? Since when was sex part of the arrangement?'

Alexa was still engaged in playing with the phone and, although she tensed at her sister's question, she did not lift her head for several seconds. Blue-green eyes scornful, she looked over at Alissa. 'Think about what you're saying. How are you planning to pretend to be his wife without ever sharing a bedroom with him?'

That angle hadn't occurred to Alissa and she compressed her lips in dismay. 'I didn't realise that the job entailed carrying on the pretence that we were a couple behind closed doors.'

'You can't be that naïve. He must have a lot of staff and he wants everyone to think it's the real deal, not just a select few. Of course what happens behind those closed doors would be your choice entirely.'

Alissa's rigid expression of disapproval had eased a little. 'So there was no *prior* assumption that there would be…er…intimacy of that nature?'

'Of course not. What do you think I am?' Alexa demanded sharply. 'But put a young and attractive man and woman in the same room and nature tends to take its course, if you know what I mean.'

The trouble was that Alissa genuinely didn't know, for she had as yet no experience to equal her twin's.

'You can't *still* be a virgin!' Alexa exclaimed, interpreting her sister's embarrassment with a look of disbelief.

In a defensive movement, Alissa threw back her slim shoulders. 'Why shouldn't I be?' she asked with quiet conviction. 'I just haven't met the right person yet and I'm not ashamed of that.'

'Sometimes I just can't believe we're twins. We are *so* different!' Alexa carolled in frustration. 'Why do you make sex such a big deal? Is it any wonder you're still on your own? A guy has to tick every box on your checklist to get anywhere near you. This exchange is just not going to work.'

'What do you mean?'

'I'm the one who was picked to be Sergei's wife and it looks like I'm the only one of us capable of carrying it off,' Alexa breathed flatly. 'Since we can't repay the money, I'll have to get an abortion.'

In horror, Alissa leapt to her feet. 'I won't let you do that!'

'We only have two options,' her twin reminded her doggedly. 'You marry him in my place so that we can keep the money, or I terminate this pregnancy and stick to the contract—'

'I *said* I would do it,' Alissa retorted, unnerved by her twin's mood, for she knew how impulsive her sister could be and she was very much afraid that Alexa might still press on with her idea of a termination.

'But you're baulking at every little thing!' Alexa flung angrily at her.

'I don't call sharing a bedroom with a guy I hardly know a "little" thing…'

'That's right, go ahead and make me feel like a total slut just because I wouldn't have made a big fuss about it when he's so gorgeous! All right, I've had a lot of men in my life and you haven't, but do you have to be so superior and smug about it?'

'I'm not superior or smug,' Alissa protested in dismay. 'Anything but!'

'Well, you'd better make your mind up fast. Do you want to help Mum or not?' Alexa demanded coldly.

And did she also want to be an aunt to the baby that her sister was carrying? Alissa added inwardly. She had met the baby's father, Harry, only that day when he'd arrived to take both young women out for lunch. Alissa had liked him very much and was satisfied that he genuinely loved her wilful twin. Right now, Alexa, however, was less easy to read or predict. Her sister was all over the place emotionally, one moment sentimental about her approaching motherhood and marriage, the next feeling threatened by the awareness that her freedom would be curtailed. Alissa could see the manner in which her twin was still retaining a possessive grip on the ridiculously expensive phone. She also knew how easily tempted her sister was by luxury goods. More than once Alexa's love of designer labels had got her into serious debt. Alissa also fully understood that, confronted by that outrageous diamond-studded phone, Alexa was wondering if she had made a serious mistake when she had surrendered the chance to marry a billionaire, regardless of how brief and fake the alliance was to be.

Alissa was determined to stay with the solution that promised her sister the best chance of happiness and she rammed down a lid on all her own reservations and breathed in deep. 'I want to help Mum more than anything. I'll go ahead with it, whatever it costs.'

CHAPTER THREE

ONLY a few hours after that conversation, Sergei snatched up a towel and strode out of the wet room where he had cooled his hot blood under a long cold shower. He snatched up a towel. It was four in the morning and he had barely slept. He had tossed and turned, as overheated and hungry for a woman as a sex-starved teenage boy. He was not amused by that reality and he was bewildered and frustrated by the sexual intensity Alissa Bartlett had fired in him.

A brooding frown stamped on his lean strong features, he logged onto his notebook PC and brought up the photo of his bride-to-be. It was a source of irritation that the woman in the picture somehow contrived both to look like Alissa and yet *not* like her. In the flesh, her face was softer, rounder, her eyes brighter, her smile full of appeal. How were those differences possible? Obviously it was an old photo, taken when she was thinner, and it wasn't a flattering representation.

Desire, however, did not blind Sergei to more obvious facts. In every way, he reflected grimly, Alissa Bartlett had proved to be much more of an unknown quantity than he'd expected. She had demonstrated quirky autonomous traits that made him distinctly uneasy. He had thought the marriage plan was pure perfection with every detail settled in advance of the ceremony and the margin for error reduced to almost nothing. He had believed she was a safe choice. But when he endeavoured to slot that defiant little blonde, who had danced with another man, into his game plan he saw dangerous ripples spreading as though a large boulder had suddenly been pitched into still water. Gut instinct now warned him that Alissa was a bad bet, more likely to give him trouble than a smooth and successful conclusion.

He should bail out now, Sergei acknowledged grittily. Unfortunately he found her hugely attractive and that advantage would be almost impossible to find elsewhere. An overlong procession of greedy, cunning lovers had made Sergei exceedingly choosy about the women he took to his bed. It was ironic that even though Alissa had infuriated him she had also ignited a stronger level of pure driven lust in him than he had experienced in over a decade.

Alissa had also resurrected his appetite for risk. So what if he was taking a chance on her? He pictured her in her little black dress, firm breasts rising above the scooped neckline in a tantalisingly voluptuous display as she spun on the dance floor, revealing glimpses of her slender thighs. His body reacted with maddening enthusiasm to the image. He had liked that dress but it would have shocked Yelena. The outfit had been too revealing for anything other than private consumption. He would have to take her shopping to ensure that she acquired more sedate clothing, while also ensuring that some day soon she would put on that dress especially for him so that he could strip it off and enjoy the delights of the body that lay underneath.

If he was so hot to taste this forbidden fruit he had to take the risk of marrying her. Such powerful desire demanded and deserved satisfaction. He was willing to sacrifice his freedom and marry to please his grandmother, but he saw no reason why he shouldn't make every effort to ensure it was, at least, a pleasurable and entertaining experience.

Alissa wakened with a start when her shoulder was roughly shaken. A phone was ringing and she sat up on the sofa, where she had spent a most uncomfortable night, and looked woozily at Alexa, who was extending her diamond-studded phone.

'Answer it, for goodness' sake!' her twin urged. 'I can't answer it for you. It's sure to be *him* and it's safer if he doesn't know I exist.'

Alissa answered the phone.

'I want to take you shopping,' Sergei announced without any preliminary greetings. 'I'll pick you up at ten.'

And that was that. It was not a request, but an order. As she shared both that opinion and the outing mentioned with her sister Alissa studied the phone with disfavour, convinced that it was more of a convenient command line for Sergei than a gift.

'Of course he's going to be bossy!' Alexa snapped crossly. 'He didn't make all that lovely cash by acting like a wimp. He's rich and powerful and he knows what he wants and when he wants it.'

'I haven't got much time. I'd better get dressed.'

Alexa released a heavy sigh of irritation. 'And I can't trust you to do it on your own.'

Her sister's annoyance permeated the atmosphere as she insisted on putting together an outfit for Alissa to wear.

'What is really wrong?' Alissa pressed anxiously.

'I feel like you're stealing my life,' Alexa confided, shocking her twin with that accusing statement. 'A billionaire is taking you shopping and it should have been me!'

Alissa gave her aggrieved sister a troubled appraisal. 'You're going to marry Harry soon. He loves you and you love him and you have a baby to look forward to. Everything with Sergei is fake and it won't last,' she reminded her.

'When I look at a photo of Sergei Antonovich I'm still jealous,' Alexa said tightly. 'And I'm not used to being jealous of you. What man ever looked at you when I was around? I've always been the prettier, more popular twin.'

The bell buzzed. Alissa was tense, hurt and nonplussed at her sister's admission. Alissa longed to suggest that Alexa take her place but, of course, that option was no longer possible. Borya accompanied Alissa downstairs. She was lost in her thoughts, acknowledging that it was true that Alexa had always enjoyed the status of being the more attractive of the two of them. She was thinner and wittier, always beautifully groomed and she drew men like bees to a honeypot. What was true now had also been true, more painfully so, in their adolescence.

Alissa winced at the secret knowledge that she had once fallen hard for their neighbour, Peter, but had never truly existed for him except as Alexa's sister and a friend. She had gone through agonies of guilt where

Peter had been concerned, because she had known that loving her sister's boyfriend was disloyal and shameful. As a result, she had never told anyone how she'd felt about Peter, not even when Alexa had deceived him with other men, revelling in the other opportunities and passing flirtations that came her way. Alexa had always had a somewhat elastic approach to fidelity, for she had reserved the right to be outraged when their father had gone off with another woman.

Alissa's train of thought was derailed with startling abruptness when she first caught sight of Sergei ensconced in the back seat of the opulent limousine. He was even bigger, darker and more gorgeous than she remembered. One glance and her mouth ran dry and a flock of butterflies broke loose in her tummy.

'Alissa.' Sergei scanned her with laser-bright dark golden eyes that missed nothing. She looked tense and miserable, which could only irritate a man accustomed to female smiles and gushing appreciation. She was dressed in yet another mistake, he noted, watching with unashamedly hypocritical male appreciation while she endeavoured to take a seat in a short tight skirt and high-heeled boots without showing him her undergarments. But, mood and wardrobe errors aside, she still looked fabulous. He was already trying to pin down exactly what he found so irresistible about her.

Was it those big aquamarine eyes that, according to the light, went from the sea-blue to mysterious, deep-forest-green? The delicacy of her bone structure? The exceptionally feminine appeal of her tiny fragile proportions? Those delightfully unexpected curves?

'Why are we going shopping?' she asked.

'You have a final fitting for your wedding dress…and I believe we should also take the opportunity to extend your wardrobe.'

Alexa had already had dress fittings? Why on earth had her twin failed to warn her of that fact? The prospect of trying on a wedding dress intimidated Alissa, while Sergei's concluding comment simply surprised her. 'But why do I need more clothes?'

'Those you wear are too revealing,' Sergei informed her bluntly.

Her face flamed as though he had turned a blowtorch on her and her fingernails dug crescents into the skin of her palms as she swallowed back a tart response. She could easily have agreed the point and it annoyed her that she could not shrug off responsibility for the outfits he had so far seen her in. Her full curves at breast and hip made fitted tops and short skirts seem much more daring than Alexa's ethereal slenderness ever had.

Sergei shifted an expressive hand. 'You look very sexy but I want a more upmarket conservative image for my wife.'

Thirty minutes later, Alissa underwent one of the most mortifying experiences of her life as the designer and her assistants endeavoured without success to get a toile—a sort of understudy to a real bridal gown—to fasten on her.

'I think I may have put on a little weight,' Alissa said tightly as their combined efforts to cram her into the too small garment were constricting her lungs.

As that confession was made the toile went slack again and her attendants backed off. An uneasy silence fell.

'I'll take your measurements again, if I may?' the designer asked with commendable brightness.

Red-faced with embarrassment and feeling the size of a heifer, Alissa withstood being measured and could not avoid seeing the designer's mounting anguish as the numbers expanded.

'Don't worry,' the older woman finally murmured with rigid calm. 'The dress will be altered in time for the ceremony.'

Alissa guessed that the lack of open lamentation was down to the small fortune that Sergei was undoubtedly paying for the gown. But she was mortified by her companions' astonishment. After all, brides usually got thinner before their weddings.

'That took a long time,' Sergei remarked when she rejoined him. He cast aside his copy of *The Financial Times* with a strong suggestion of relief.

'The dress will have to be altered,' she admitted.

Sergei frowned, black brows pleating in surprise. 'You've lost weight?'

Biting at her lower lip, Alissa said the only thing she felt she could say in the circumstances. 'No, I've put it on. I'll have to starve from now on—'

'Not while you're with me, *milaya moya*,' Sergei quipped. 'I won't allow you to shrink your assets.'

It was impossible not to notice his downward glance that paid homage to the swell of her breasts beneath the sweater she wore. In receipt of that all-too-male look of appreciation, Alissa went so red she was vaguely surprised she didn't spontaneously combust. 'I like food too much, particularly chocolate,' she heard herself respond inanely while she strove valiantly to ignore the sexual spark in the atmosphere.

It was a novelty for Sergei to be with a woman who

admitted to enjoying food. He was more accustomed to ladies who demanded the calorie count of a dish before they would even consider eating.

Back in the limo, Alissa wondered how on earth he managed to make her so painfully aware of him as a man. Or was she oversensitive to his potent male aura? Whatever, she was conscious of every breath he drew.

In yet another exclusive designer salon they were served with champagne while a large collection of clothes was presented for scrutiny. Alissa tried on a scarlet dress and jacket. It was a perfect fit and very much more conventional in style than anything her sister would have chosen. Feeling ridiculously self-conscious, she emerged from the cubicle to let Sergei see it. He, she was starting to appreciate, liked to be in charge more than was good for him *or* her.

'I like that,' he breathed in sudden amusement. 'Add some fur and you could be a very cute female Santa Claus…'

'No fur, please,' she replied, then queried, 'Do you have Santa Claus in Russia?'

'*Ded Moroz*…Grandfather Frost, and he comes in the New Year with a female sidekick called the Snowmaiden,' Sergei told her. 'But you can celebrate Christmas any way you want while you're with me. I didn't even know the festival existed until I went to live with my grandmother.'

While you're with me; a subtle little reminder that she would be a temporary wife rather than a real one, Alissa assumed. Christmas was only seven weeks away. Where would she be living then? Feeling extraordinarily vulnerable, she stood still while his smouldering dark eyes raked over her. An inner glow spread through her pelvis, tightening her tummy muscles and leaving her insanely aware of his raw sexual power.

At his behest, she tried on outfit after outfit. Half the time he was on the phone, delivering terse commands in his own language, but the whole time his attention seemed to be on her. It bothered her that she got a thrill out of his obvious interest and she had to resist a shameful urge to preen and pose. It was becoming harder and harder for her to view their approaching marriage as just a job, since he was personalising everything. An hour after their arrival, a package was delivered to him by his chauffeur.

Alissa made her final appearance in an opulent full length turquoise silk evening gown.

One glance at her and the exquisite pain of rampant sexual arousal assailed Sergei in a tidal wave. The fabric cupping her breasts was too fine to conceal her nipples which protruded like ripe cherries. Expelling his breath in a slow hiss of restraint, he sprang upright and signalled her.

'Come here,' he told her when she stopped a few feet away from him.

With care, Sergei employed a tissue to wipe her lips clear of tinted gloss. 'Less is more,' he murmured in a roughened undertone.

Alissa gazed up at him wide-eyed and was ludicrously unprepared for the kiss that followed. Long fingers meshing with her hair, he pried her lips apart and took her mouth with erotic force. His hunger exploded through her and her head spun and her stomach lurched with excitement as if she were on a fairground ride. The tight knot in her tummy clenched hard and with every fibre of her being she craved more intimate contact.

'Right moment, wrong place, *milaya*,' Sergei quipped, setting her back from him, and she almost screamed and stamped her foot with frustration. While he called every shot and maintained supremacy, he also made her feel controlled and helpless. Nothing, it seemed, took the edge off her intense craving for him. 'Open your mouth.'

'Why?' she framed stonily, annoyed that he had kissed her again and left her feeling things she barely understood and certainly didn't want to feel. Her body was humming and all churned up in a very uncomfortable way.

'You can't have me right now but you can have... *this*,' he murmured playfully, sliding a chocolate between her lips.

The meltingly rich taste of chocolate reached Alissa's taste buds in a gastronomic tide of sensation. It tasted so good, she almost closed her eyes to savour it in full. 'That is to die for,' she whispered.

Sergei got an erotic buzz just watching her. She was a wonderfully sensual woman and she could wind him up like a clock. He wanted to scoop her up into his arms and take her somewhere private where he could sink deep and hard and repeatedly into her lush little body until he had satisfied the fierce hunger he was restraining with such difficulty. But on another level he was enjoying that unusual edge of anticipation driven by a level of moderation he had never practised before.

Somewhere close by a phone rang insistently. Alissa broke free of the spell holding her in stasis. 'That's mine.'

One of the assistants brought her the mobile phone from the changing room. It was Alexa calling, words gushing from her in a breathless tide. 'Mum's found out that you're marrying Sergei next week. One of her friends brought in a newspaper with a picture of you together. She's in deep shock—'

'Oh, my word,' Alissa exclaimed in consternation, uneasily conscious of Sergei's proximity. 'What did you tell her?'

'Well, that you'd been seeing Sergei when you were still working in London but that it hadn't worked out and that's why you never mentioned him,' Alexa explained. 'And now he's back and it's all on again. What else could I say?'

'This just goes on getting more and more complicated,' Alissa lamented.

'What's going on?' Sergei demanded, and one glance at his lean, taut features was sufficient to tell her how much he hated being left out of the loop on any issue.

'My mother saw a photo of us together in a newspaper and she's in shock—'

'Is that her you're speaking to? No?' he queried. 'Then get her on the phone so that I can speak to her.'

And although Alissa tried to argue with him, nothing else would satisfy him. Alissa dialled the number of her home and broke through her mother's anxious and reproachful questions to ask her to speak to Sergei. Sergei then took the phone from her damp grasp and proceeded to stun Alissa by selling himself as the perfect son-in-law, who couldn't wait to meet his future mother-in-law. While Alissa hovered, taut with growing incredulity and resentment at the ease with which he dealt with the situation, he insisted he would send a car to pick her parent up and ferry her back to London to dine with them that same evening.

When he had finished talking, he passed the phone back to Alissa.

'I do understand why you got swept away by him,' Jenny Bartlett told her daughter in a dazed voice. 'Sergei really *does* know what he wants, doesn't he? I can't wait to meet him, darling.'

'I seem to recall that your parents are getting a divorce,' Sergei remarked when the call had finished.

'Yes,' Alissa confirmed with a flat lack of expression, shying away from that controversial subject while dimly also wondering why he had never known about Christmas until he went to live with his grandmother. Had his parents died? What age had he been? She decided it was no business of hers and that if she wanted to survive their fake marriage she had to learn to keep a sensible distance from him.

She didn't go back to Alexa's flat that evening. Meanwhile, Sergei dropped her off at his indescribably chic apartment to get changed while he returned to his office to attend a meeting. Alissa wandered round the penthouse admiring the fabulous art works on display, before selecting an elegant green shift dress to wear. The prospect of trying to deceive her mother into crediting that she was in love with Sergei seriously unnerved her.

But she need not have worried for right from the start Sergei took centre stage and it was soon clear that her mother was much impressed by his calm and assurance. Alissa, however, was taken aback when the older woman let drop that Alexa had picked the same day to marry Harry that Alissa had to marry Sergei. As quickly Alissa assumed that Alexa had chosen that date deliberately to ensure that Sergei did not have an opportunity to meet her.

'An extraordinary coincidence,' Sergei commented.

'A disaster because I can't be in two places at once,' Alissa's mother opined in a pained voice, her distress unconcealed at that clash of dates. 'I'm heavily involved in organising Alexa's day and, because she's pregnant, I can't possibly abandon her to see to it all on her own—'

'Of course not,' Alissa broke in and squeezed her mother's hand soothingly. 'We understand…'

'But I really would like to see both my daughters get married.'

'Unhappily our arrangements are too advanced to allow the date to be changed,' Sergei said in a tone of apology.

'But there is a solution,' Jenny told him hopefully. 'Would you consider a double wedding with Alexa and Harry here in the UK?'

Alissa's eyes opened very wide at that startling suggestion and she froze in dismay; if Sergei met her sister, he would learn that Jenny's daughters were identical twins and he might well become suspicious!

'I'm afraid such an arrangement would not be possible.' Sergei then explained that he had an elderly and frail grandmother who had never left Russia in her life and who was eagerly looking forward to attending their traditional wedding in St Petersburg.

Alissa assumed it was a polite lie, but she was impressed by his inventiveness when put on the spot. She reckoned that the presence of her mother at her own bogus wedding would only make the occasion more of a strain. When it occurred to her that she was already in the very act of deceiving her mother, guilt pierced her deep.

Sergei then went on to suggest that he and Alissa should have a church blessing, followed by a party at which he could meet Alissa's friends and family, in London the following month. Her mother's disappointed face slowly warmed to that prospect and it was easy to tell from the suggestions she went on to make for the event that she was, not only charmed by the idea, but also equally charmed by the man who had voiced it.

When the meal was over, Alissa opted to return home with her mother. Sergei's steely glance warned her that he was displeased by that choice, but Alissa had no intention of spending time alone with him at his penthouse. Their marriage was supposed to be a legal arrangement and a job, nothing more, and if she wanted him to respect those boundaries she needed to keep some distance between them. In addition, Alissa was in no hurry to return to Alexa's apartment laden with piles of expensive clothes that would be likely to awaken her twin's bitter envy again.

'I expected to see you again before the wedding,' Sergei revealed, standing on the pavement beside the Mercedes that contained Alissa's mother and awaited Alissa.

'I'm sorry—I'd like to spend some time at home before I go to Russia.' Pale and taut, Alissa collided head on with smouldering dark golden eyes heavily fringed with lush black lashes. Her tummy flipped as if she had been flung up in the air. Surely no man had ever had such compellingly beautiful eyes? Her fingers clenched into her palms as she stepped back from Sergei, uneasily aware of the phalanx of bodyguards hovering around them.

'You make it sound so reasonable, *milaya*.' Sergei reached out and closed a hand round hers as she brushed a skein of gold silky hair back from her brow. He eased her inexorably closer. 'But you know that's not what I want.'

The lashes above her aquamarine eyes fluttered down to conceal her strained gaze. Her heart was racing like an overwound clock behind her breastbone. His mesmeric pull was almost more than she could bear. Even the timbre of his rich dark drawl slivered through her like the lick of a flame. But that tide of physical response infuriated her and stung her pride.

'Surely there's some part of the day when I can have my own free time?' Alissa queried, throwing her blonde head high, a gleam of challenge in her bright eyes.

'Your own free time?' Sergei countered, his lean dark features tensing.

'Isn't this a job? I can't be on duty twenty-four-seven.'

Sergei froze, all warmth ebbing from his gaze leaving it winter-dark and cold. In that instant she could have done nothing more offensive than voice a cool and emotionless reminder of the legal agreement that had brought them together He marvelled that for a little while he had somehow contrived to forget that fact. Her words had grated on him, striking the hard calculating note that he was all too accustomed to hearing from her sex. Evidently he had not yet been generous enough to keep her sweet.

'I don't think you can have read the small print on your contract,' he breathed in an icy cutting tone of distaste. 'From the moment you wear my wedding ring, you *will* be on duty twenty-four-seven.'

Sergei walked away, leaving Alissa paralysed on the pavement with nervous tension. She was torn between regret and relief. A terrifying part of her wanted to run after him, to douse the aggression she had awakened and luxuriate in the kiss that she had subconsciously longed to receive. But the rest of her rejoiced in saying no to that weaker part of her nature. She wasn't a toy for him to play with as and when he fancied. She was too proud and intelligent to behave like the women who had fawned on him at his club the night when they'd first met, wasn't she? But just at that moment pride was a cold companion filling her with disappointment rather than a sense of achievement…

CHAPTER FOUR

WHEN Alissa returned from her walk, Alexa, her face flushed with annoyance, pounced on her twin the moment she entered the house. 'Where have you been?'

'You were still in bed when I got up. I had a few things to buy and then I went for a walk...'

'A walk?' Alexa wailed in disbelief. 'You're flying to Russia this afternoon and all you can think to do with yourself is go for a stupid walk?'

Alissa compressed her lips. 'I don't know how long I'll be away. I'll miss this place.'

'Mum came home at lunchtime. She's guessed where we got the money from!' her sister told her abruptly.

Alissa studied her twin in dismay. 'How could she possibly have guessed?'

'Naturally she doesn't know about the marriage-as-a-job angle,' Alexa breathed impatiently. 'But even though I'm the one who gave the money to the solicitor, she's convinced that *you* must have got the money from Sergei to pay off Dad.'

Alissa groaned. 'My goodness, how am I supposed to talk my way out of that?'

'Well, you don't need to bother. Sergei's loaded and

he's about to become Mum's son-in-law and one of the family. I said that he'd given the money to you and it was up to you what you did with it. I talked her out of phoning him to discuss it.'

Alexa's ability to talk her way out of a tight corner was legendary. Alissa regarded her with wry bemusement.

Her twin widened scornful aquamarine eyes. 'So once again, *you* didn't need to do anything; *I* saved the day.'

Anger flashed through Alissa and she had to grit her teeth to hold it back. In spite of the fact that Alexa was marrying Harry in twenty-four hours, her sister was behaving as though she were the wronged party. 'No, I'm the one saving the day this time around,' Alissa contradicted. 'You signed the contract in my name without my knowledge, but I'm marrying Sergei.'

'Whoopee-do, and what a sacrifice that is!' Alexa exclaimed with stinging derision. 'He's absolutely gorgeous, fantastically rich and incredibly generous. Look at the presents he keeps on sending you, never mind the flowers! Anyone would be forgiven for thinking you're marrying him for real tomorrow.'

Her face tight with discomfiture, Alissa went upstairs to escape the argument. It hurt to be at odds with her twin, to be forced to accept that Alexa's love of money and luxury currently seemed more important to her than Harry, or even her baby. Over the past five days, Sergei had sent Alissa flowers every morning as well as several unexpected gifts. Alissa wondered if he was trying to convince her mother that they were a normal bride and groom, for she couldn't think of any other reason for his munificence. She was now the bemused owner of a diamond-studded watch, an extensive set of designer luggage and a diamond solitaire ring that had made Alexa so jealous she had snapped at Harry when he had collected her for their wedding rehearsal that same evening.

Was Sergei simply getting into the role of keen bridegroom? He had phoned her every day as well. But he talked as though words came at a premium price that he was too stingy to pay. He would mention briefly that he was in New York or had just closed a deal, or he would talk about his football club or the players. Alissa found herself chattering about nothing in particular to fill the awkward lulls and afterwards she would cringe at the memory of her more inane comments. And, sometimes, Sergei would ask questions that were more terrifying than encouraging.

'How many men have you had in your life?' had been one blunt and bold enquiry that had shaken her.

'One or two,' she had told him grudgingly and, to punish him for his inappropriate curiosity, she had counter-attacked with, 'Have you ever been in love?'

'That is when you get excessively attached to one woman? No, I've never even come close,' he had informed her with a distinct note of satisfaction, as if falling in love was something *real* men didn't do.

'Then why did you get married that first time?' she had heard herself demand before she could think better of getting so personal—especially when she was trying to set an example by being impersonal with him.

A yawning, uneasy silence had greeted her query.

'She was the most beautiful woman I had ever seen,' he had finally imparted in a discouragingly gritty response. *But that's so superficial,* Alissa had wanted to tell him, though the tense atmosphere had kept her quiet.

Those phone conversations had brought Alissa no nearer to knowing the man she had agreed to marry. If anything he had become more of an enigma than ever. He could be very unpredictable. He was still a closed book in every way that mattered and curiosity was starting to kill her. She needed to know what made Sergei Antonovich tick, what made him angry, what made him happy. With each day that passed the big black hole of her ignorance only irritated her more.

That afternoon, Alissa parted from her mother and her sister in the privacy of their home. Alexa was brittle and moody and Alissa wished her twin and her prospective bridegroom well before she left alone for the airport. Of course, while she was involved with Sergei she could never be truly alone, because he had insisted that she accept the presence of a pair of bodyguards, who had collected her from home.

Her mobile phone rang on the journey. When she answered it, she was taken aback to hear her father's voice. 'Your mother told me at the weekend that you're leaving this afternoon. I'm at the airport and I need to talk to you—'

'At the airport?' Alissa repeated in surprise.

'Meet me for coffee,' Maurice Bartlett urged. 'I'm only here to see you. It feels like half a lifetime since we last met.'

The formalities of travel complete, Alissa, a slim elegant figure clad in a full length black coat and boots, went to meet her father. When he saw her he rose from his table and hurried into the concourse to greet her. As he approached her her bodyguards came between them.

'It's okay. I know him. You can take a break,' Alissa

urged her bodyguards in some embarrassment, making vague shooing motions with her hands as if she were dealing with a flock of hens.

The two men exchanged uneasy glances and backed off with reluctance. Appraising her troubled face with a frown, Maurice Bartlett closed both his hands round hers as if he feared she might suddenly decide to walk off again. He was a handsome blond man who looked a good deal younger than his age. 'Thanks for coming. I knew you couldn't be as hard and unforgiving as your sister has been.'

'I'm not forgiving you for the past six months—just now I couldn't,' Alissa admitted gruffly half under her breath. 'But you're still my father.'

'I can't believe how long it's been since I saw you.'

She was appalled to feel a surge of childish tears sting her eyes. 'That's not my fault. You left us—'

'No, I didn't. I left your mother,' he argued, wrapping his arms round her to pull her close as her tears over-flowed and rolled down her cheeks. 'I can't bear to lose you and Alexa as well. These last months haven't been easy for me either—'

He urged her into a seat and sped off to get coffee. Being with him felt wrong to Alissa, like straying into the enemy camp. The pain he had caused all of them was still too fresh. She breathed in deep and blinked back the tears, hoping that her mascara was waterproof.

Her father sat down beside her and gripped her hand in his. 'If it makes you feel any better, it's not working out with Maggie,' he confided heavily.

Alissa swallowed hard, for that news was not a comfort. It only made her wonder if all the heartbreak had been for nothing. 'I've only got a few minutes,' she warned him.

'So how did you fall in love with a billionaire?' he quipped. 'Now if it had been your sister, I would have been less surprised.'

Alissa was grateful for the abrupt change of subject. 'Harry, Alexa's man, is lovely. He adores her.'

'For his own sake, I hope he can stand up to her as well. Alexa's headstrong and I can't quite picture her settling down to be a wife and mother,' the older man confided ruefully.

Alissa looked at her father and without even meaning to heard herself say accusingly, 'We used to be such a happy family.' As soon as she said it and saw him recoil guiltily, the tears welled up in her eyes again. Both happy and sad memories tore at her. She would never have dreamt that the breakdown of her parents' marriage would cause her so much grief as an adult.

She was swallowing back a sob when she noticed a pair of photographers standing nearby with cameras angled in their direction. Anxiety gripped her because Sergei had warned her that she needed to be on the lookout for the paparazzi now to avoid them. 'I've got to go,' she said abruptly and stood up.

Her father hugged her and dropped a kiss on the top of her head. 'I'm sorry,' he said despondently. 'I'm really sorry. Sometimes you don't know what you have until you lose it.'

Alissa eased gently free again. Moisture still glittering on her pale cheeks, she moved away, noting the relief of her security team as they fell in either side of her. Her father was a weak man who didn't seem to know what he wanted any more. Only a couple of months ago he had told them all that he could not live without Maggie Lines and that he had to be with her. Did he want to go back to her mother now? Or was that a fanciful idea?

Alissa's first experience of travelling in a private jet soothed her fractured emotions. She revelled in the peace and tranquillity and all the space while the cabin crew attended to her every need. She watched a film and skimmed through several glossy magazines before enjoying a very pleasant meal followed by a box of Belgian chocolates, which she found impossible to resist. She had one chocolate and closed the box feeling very virtuous, but was eventually tempted into eating more. Sergei phoned her during the flight.

'Thanks for the chocs,' she murmured, 'but I shouldn't be thanking you, I should be complaining. I've already eaten half of them.'

'Didn't I tell you that I'm fattening you up for Christmas?' Sergei teased.

'That's not a joke, Sergei. When it comes to chocolate you have to be cruel to be kind,' she warned him. 'I'm not great with will power.'

'I have a meeting this evening, so I won't see you before the ceremony,' he told her.

Stark disappointment flashed through Alissa and took her very much by surprise. Why was it that she had to constantly remind herself that she was deceiving her family to play a paid role in Sergei's life? Why did she keep on forgetting that basic fact? Why the heck couldn't she stop thinking about Sergei Antonovich? What was she? An immature adolescent or an adult? His attraction ought to be outweighed by his 'Neanderthal man' approach to women, she told herself sternly.

Mid-evening the jet landed at Pulkovo Airport in St Petersburg. It was much colder than it had been in London. A limo wafted her slowly through the city streets. She had never seen so many fabulous old buildings grouped in one place, so she was less surprised than she might have been when she was deposited outside a splendid classical property and informed that she had arrived at Scrgei's home. She mounted the steps, her breath like puffs of smoke in the icy air, and walked into the merciful warmth of a superb big hallway with an intricate polished wooden floor. The lemon-coloured walls, stucco work and restrained furnishings were supremely elegant and quite unexpected after the edgy modern design of Scrgci's London apartment.

The stylish décor continued upstairs and into the green and gold guest room where her luggage was deposited. She turned down the offer of food and stifled a yawn. It had been a long day and she was very tired. A pair of maids arrived to unpack for her and she took refuge from all the attention in the stunning bathroom. Lying back in the hot water while jets pummelled her weary limbs was wonderfully relaxing and she stayed there longer than she had planned and indeed was beginning to drift off to sleep when a loud rata-tat-tat sounded on the door and made her sit up with a start.

'Yes?' she called in dismay, clumsily scrambling up and clambering out to grab a towel.

'It's Sergei…I want to speak to you.'

Aquamarine eyes flying wide with surprise in her flushed face, Alissa snatched the white towelling robe off the back of the door and hastily put it on. It was not a flattering garment but it was better than a bath towel.

Barefoot and hesitant, she emerged, feeling naked without her make-up on. She had not even had the time to run a brush through the tousled damp hair she had piled on top of her head.

One glance at Sergei, looking impossibly tall and intimidating as he strode forward, stole the breath from her lungs. In a charcoal-grey business suit, he was a spectacular sight, but his expression paralysed her in her tracks. His lean, darkly handsome face was hard and taut with anger as he slung a couple of photographs down on the bed in an aggressive gesture. 'Explain yourself!'

Stiff with astonishment, Alissa collided with scorching dark golden eyes and then bemusedly turned her attention to the pictures on the bed. She moved closer and frowned down at the grainy images, her bewilderment only increasing when she realised that they depicted her with her father at the airport café. 'What is there to explain?'

Sergei dealt her a look of pure black fury that made her lose colour. 'How can you ask me that?' he seethed in a raw undertone.

Alissa went rigid with indignation at his attitude. 'Don't you dare raise your voice to me!' she launched back at him angrily.

Sergei surveyed her in disbelief. 'Is that all you have to say to me?'

Alissa shrugged, strands of golden hair sliding down from her topknot to curve to her pink cheeks. 'I've got nothing at all to say to you. You barge in here when I'm in the bath—'

'I knocked on the door!' Sergei grated.

'The very fact that you think that that is something to boast about says it all really, doesn't it?' Treating him to a disdainful look that would have shrivelled a less assured male, Alissa carefully worked her way round to the other side of the bed. 'How dare you shout at me?'

'If I see you holding hands with another man and weeping over him, shouting is the very least of what you can expect from me!' he raked back at her without hesitation, clearing the foot of the bed in one long stride to close the distance between them again.

'I will not be threatened.' Breathing in short agitated bursts, Alissa reached for the crystal vase of flowers on the occasional table beside her. 'If you come one step closer to me, I will thump you with this!'

His ebony brows snapped together in a smouldering frown of incredulity. 'Are you crazy?'

'I can look after myself,' Alissa declared with bristling outrage.

'Why the hell would you try to thump me?' Sergei demanded. 'I'm not threatening you with violence.'

Alissa made no attempt to loosen her white-knuckled hold on the vase. *'No?'*

Sobered and set back by that condemnation, Sergei looked grave. 'Of course, I'm not. I would never hurt a woman.' He reached down faster than she could react and deftly removed the vase from her hand to set it back on the table. 'You scare really easily, don't you?'

'And you're *surprised*?' Alissa bawled back at him full volume, rage and embarrassment combining inside her. 'You roar in here like a hurricane…'

With a ground-out curse in Russian beneath his

breath, Sergei snatched up one of the photos. 'Stop trying to avoid the issue. Who is this man?'

Alissa tightened the belt on her towelling wrap and folded her arms. 'My father—'

'Don't tell me a stupid lie like that!' Sergei snapped, out of all patience at that response as he stared down at the photo in his hand. 'This man looks no older than I am—'

'I'm sure Dad would be very flattered to hear that opinion, but I'm just bored with the whole subject. Why don't you check your facts before you attack people?'

'I don't make a habit of attacking people,' Sergei asserted grimly, well aware that for once in his life he had let his temper rip before he had investigated the cold hard facts. That was not how he usually operated and he could not explain the sudden absence of logic and cool that had afflicted him. He only knew that he felt out of kilter and that made him uneasy. 'If that man is your father, why are you holding his hand and crying?'

'It was an emotional moment and I hadn't seen him or talked to him for weeks.' Alissa was still angry with Sergei and she shot the crystal vase a look of regret, for thumping him with it might have released some of her pent-up fury. 'Going by the way you're behaving, you're obviously used to women who play around behind your back—'

'I am not,' Sergei cut in to dismiss that insulting charge while wondering why the instant he saw those photos of her with another man a red mist of rage had enveloped him to the exclusion of every other thought and prompting.

'You're not even my boyfriend,' Alissa pointed out.

'But tomorrow I will be your husband—'

'I hope you'll forgive me for saying that right at

this moment that doesn't strike me as a very appealing prospect,' Alissa retorted with a challenging lift of her chin.

'I'm not trying to appeal to you.' Aggressive to the last, Sergei flung his arrogant dark head high. 'I am what I am and I'm unlikely to change.'

'Well, that's certainly telling me, isn't it?' Alissa quipped. 'You're not even bright enough to learn from your mistakes.'

The silence screamed. His lean, powerful length taut with shock at that comeback, Sergei viewed her with burning disbelief.

Conscience smote Alissa. Why was it that when she began fighting with him she could never resist the urge to top his last remark? It was a bad habit and a dismal way to embark on their relationship; he would keep on fighting because he didn't know any other way. 'That was rude, not a fair comment—'

'When was a woman ever fair?' Sergei drawled between clenched teeth of outrage.

'Giving me another opening like that is just asking for trouble,' Alissa warned him ruefully, gazing at him and silently marvelling at the lush black luxuriance of the lashes that accentuated his beautiful dark eyes. 'Okay, I'm at fault for not just giving you a straight answer.'

Sergei had never met a woman capable of giving him a straight answer and he was grudgingly amused by that statement.

'But obviously my dad is my dad and I couldn't credit that anyone would think we might be a couple,' she protested in her own defence. 'And since my parents broke up, my relationship with him has really suffered, so it was a very emotional meeting.' Her throat thickened and her voice wobbled a little on that admission.

'Why?'

'Why?' Alissa wailed, bewildered by the question.

'You're an adult. What your parents do is their business.'

'Maybe you're not from a close family but we *were* really close and loving,' Alissa countered thickly, appalled to hear tears clogging her diction again and wondering when she had turned into such a watering pot. 'And then it all just went within twenty-four hours. It was such a shock. Dad announced that he'd fallen in love with another woman and, a few hellish weeks later, he moved in with her...'

With a sense of wonderment, Sergei stared down at the twin tracks of tears glistening on her cheeks. She was so emotional and that contradicted her psychological profile. She also seemed to sympathise with everyone *but* him. She'd gone from shouting at him to threatening him with a vase. His hard mouth curved ever so lightly at that comical recollection and he bent down suddenly and scooped her up easily into his arms.

'What are you doing?' Alissa yelped, fingers clutching wildly at a broad shoulder for balance.

'I think it's called being supportive. I'm not sure. It's not a field I'm experienced in,' Sergei confided, settling down on the bed with her slight frame cradled on his lap and deciding that, after all, there was something to be said for this supportive stuff.

'Mum's so unhappy and I can't fix it,' Alissa mumbled tearfully, wiping angrily at her wet eyes, finally acknowledging that she was exhausted by the day she had endured.

'She'll meet someone else and be happy again,' Sergei forecast, lowering his handsome dark head, nostrils flaring as he breathed in the soapy, peachy aroma of her hair and skin. The neckline of the robe had dropped lower and wider to reveal the smooth, tantalising upper slope of her firm breasts. That view stoked his hunger for her by a factor of ten.

'She loves Dad. Life's not that simple…'

'Only because you want to make it complicated,' Sergei cut in, tilting her head back and nuzzling his darkly shadowed jaw rhythmically against the tender skin of her throat. She quivered in his grasp, every sense leaping into sudden awareness. '*Ti takaya nezhnaya…* you are so soft, *milaya moya.*'

Alissa knew she had to pull away and respect the boundaries that she knew she needed to impose with him, but the physical ability to resist Sergei's dark allure was terrifyingly absent. He was being so gentle and she sensed that that didn't come naturally to him. Her nipples were tingling into straining prominence, sending an electrifying message to the swelling dampening tissue between her thighs. That sensual awakening was an exquisite pain.

His mouth closed over hers in a wildly intoxicating kiss. Fireworks of response blazed inside her, sending her temperature rocketing while her hunger climbed. She let her fingers sink into his cropped black hair with a muffled moan of satisfaction. She couldn't get close enough to him. He felt as necessary to her as air to breathe. The fierce intensity of his hard mouth on hers was devastatingly erotic. He slid his hand through the gaping neckline of her robe and captured a pouting rose-tipped breast, skilled fingers stroking the velvety tip into throbbing rigidity. A gasp of response erupted from her as sensation piled on sensation. He kissed her breathless and her heart was hammering so hard she felt dizzy and clung to him.

The buzz of a mobile phone proved to be the wake-up call she needed. She pushed him away with both hands and tugged the edges of the robe back together. Trembling, she slid back to the floor, shunning the bed and him and the deceptive intimacy that had almost betrayed her. He answered his phone, his dark drawl rough-edged with huskiness.

When the dialogue finished, she breathed, 'What happened to the meeting you said you had this evening?'

'A London tabloid newspaper editor sent me those photos, obviously in the hope that I would dump you and call off the wedding and so give them an even bigger scoop,' he explained with rich cynicism. 'I skipped the meeting.'

Her body was a riot of nerve-endings sizzling with a sense of loss and disappointment. He was making her want things she had never wanted before and he was teaching her to want him with a depth of longing that physically hurt. The atmosphere was explosive, undertones swirling beneath the uneasy silence that intimidated her.

Sergei always played it cool, but he was fighting a very powerful urge to just yank her back into his arms. He hated the idea that she had any kind of a hold on him, for that was not his style. 'You want me to leave,' he murmured.

Alissa stared back at him, knowing that that was not what she wanted at all, but also that it was what she should want. His lean, darkly beautiful features dazzled her, commanded her attention, and locked her gaze to him. His very interest thrilled her and made her feel special. He was the sort of guy she had never expected to meet and she knew she would never meet his like again. To be an object of desire to a male who had been with some of the world's most beautiful women just blew her away.

'Alissa..?' he prompted.

'Yes.' The word of rejection was forced from her by fear, for she felt insanely out of her depth.

As self-assured as ever, Sergei strolled over to her and rested a lean bronzed forefinger against the pulse flickering below the pale purplish hollow of her collarbone, betraying her tension. 'Tomorrow, you will be mine. Twenty- four-seven, *milaya moya*,' he reminded her silkily. 'I can hardly wait.'

Even after the door thudded shut on his departure, Alissa stayed where she was, frozen between consternation and anticipation. Some minutes later she got into bed in a daze and tried to find sleep rather than relive the forbidden delight of his hands on her body...

CHAPTER FIVE

ALISSA WAS WAKENED early the following morning and treated to breakfast in bed. Her mother phoned her to wish her well. In the background she could hear a hubbub of bridal activity and she was hurt when Alexa professed to be too busy to come to the phone and speak to her sister personally.

After she'd had a shower, Alissa found a beautician and a hairdresser awaiting her. Clearly, a strict schedule was being observed. The professionals took charge and her hair was styled, her nails painted and her face made up. She could not escape the surreal sense that none of what was happening really had anything to do with her. It was not until the wedding gown was reverently brought in by one of the designer's assistants that she began to feel involved and intimidated at one and the same time.

The white dress was an elegant column design, lifted into the extraordinary by the shimmering crystals that glittered on the gorgeous fabric like thousands of stars below the lights. Alissa was hugely impressed and equally so with the cobweb-fine lingerie and the shoes ornamented with pearls. She suffered a moment's fear that the dress would not fit, but it skimmed her curves to perfection and she dared to breathe again. The delicate tulle veil falling from the wreath of real flowers encircling her head was very pretty. When she finally saw herself in a mirror, she knew she had never looked better.

She was ushered downstairs and tucked into a limousine. When she was deposited in front of a public building, she had to fight the urge to shiver in the icy air. A young woman, who spoke fluent English, greeted her in the busy hallway and introduced herself as Lukina, one of Sergei's aides.

'Where are we?' Alissa asked.

'ZAGS—where the civil ceremony takes place.' The question seemed to surprise the brunette. 'Didn't you receive the information I sent you a few weeks ago? It contained a complete breakdown of everything that would be happening today as well as some useful pointers.'

Alissa reddened and realised that once again her twin had neglected to keep her up to speed on things that she needed to know. 'Sorry, I forgot.'

'Mr Antonovich is keen for you to make a particular effort to be pleasant to his grandmother, Yelena,' Lukina informed her anxiously. 'He's her only grandson and this is a very special day for her.'

Alissa's flush deepened at the offensive suggestion that she might have to be told to be nice to Sergei's grandmother. So it was that her eyes were sparkling when she entered the room where the ceremony was to take place. Bridal music was playing in the background as, heartbreakingly handsome in a superbly tailored dark suit, Sergei strode up to her and presented her with a dainty bouquet of rosebuds that was incongruous in his large hands and which he patently could not wait to relinquish.

Every choice concerning the wedding had been based on what Yelena might like or expect. Sergei had ordered an extremely feminine and romantic wedding dress, as he had guessed that Yelena, who had never enjoyed frills in her own life, would enjoy such a spectacle. What he had not foreseen was how well the shimmering dress and simple floral wreath would frame and enhance Alissa's fair, delicate beauty. She looked like a fairy princess from an old storybook, and although he wanted to laugh at that comparison he was disturbed by the discovery that he could not take his eyes off her.

Meeting Sergei's dark smouldering gaze, Alissa tensed. Sexual awareness and the first renewed flickers of desire stole back into her slender body. He reached for her hand and she saw a small elderly woman in a bright blue dress and jacket keenly observing them and smiled, immediately guessing who she was.

The brief ceremony was highlighted by an exchange of wedding rings and she learned that in Russia the wedding ring was worn on a woman's right hand. Afterwards they signed the register, whereupon Sergei introduced her to the woman she had noticed earlier. Yelena, as cheerful as a spring flower in her suit, glowed with energy and good humour.

Yelena shared the limousine that ferried them to the church and Sergei translated his grandmother's rapid-fire questions.

Asked if she liked children, Alissa declared that she adored them and hoped to have two or three. Yelena followed up that response with others of a more housewifely note. Did she cook? Yes, but she didn't bake very well. Did she sew? Not really, the ability to sew on a button was Alissa's only talent in that field. Did she embroider or knit? No, she didn't embroider, but she had loved knitting ever since she created tiny garments for a friend's baby. Sergei was accustomed to women without domestic skills and he was quick to assume that Alissa had decided to lie to impress Yelena. But struggling to translate a more technical exchange on knitting for the women's benefit, he began to doubt that conviction and he was pleased to see his grandmother beaming at his chosen bride.

'She took the trouble to knit for her friend's baby. That's a good woman. You've done well,' Yelena pronounced with approval, straightening her grandson's tie for him before he could assist her from the car. 'She's very pretty as well. Give as much time to your marriage as you give to business and you will be together for a lifetime.'

Taken aback by that blunt advice on how to hold onto a woman when he had much more trouble getting rid of them, Sergei escorted his bride and his grandmother into the church, which was packed with guests. Awesomely aware of being the centre of attention and recognising the buzz of curiosity as she passed by, Alissa was tense and nervous and very much afraid of making a wrong move in public. She was also striving to understand why Alexa had begged her to marry Sergei in her place while withholding all useful information about the role. Had her sister secretly wanted her twin to fall flat on her face?

The priest blessed their rings and they were given candles to hold. They held hands as the slow ritual proceeded, reaching its climax when they were crowned and followed by the sharing of a cup of wine and a final blessing.

'I really, *really* feel married after all that palaver,' Sergei growled like a bear on the way out again.

'You've been through it all before,' Alissa pointed out, less comfortable with the knowledge that she was faking a marriage in the aftermath of a solemn religious service.

'I only went through a civil ceremony the last time. This day will last for ever,' Sergei groaned. 'We still have the reception to get through.'

'Don't you enjoy socialising?' Alissa was wryly amused by his mood and grateful she was not a genuine bride, liable to feel hurt by his indifferent attitude.

'That's not the problem.' In the rear seat of the limo, Sergei gripped her hand to turn her round to face him. Black-lashed, dark golden eyes raked hungrily over her in a look that was purebred primitive. 'You make the most exquisite bride. I just want all the show and fuss to be over quickly so that I can be alone with you, *milaya moya*.'

Her face warmed, and habit almost made her voice a protest to remind him that she was only a fake bride and that his being alone with her wasn't about to change anything. But when she looked at his devastatingly handsome features and felt the pull of his potent masculinity, her heartbeat hammered in her eardrums and the griping words shrivelled on her tongue and died in her throat. The truth was that Sergei Antonovich absolutely mesmerised her and, even though she knew that the relationship could go nowhere, temptation was biting deeply into her resolve to keep things platonic.

After all, no man had ever made her feel the way Sergei made her feel and it was perfectly possible, given the level of Sergei's attraction, that no other man ever

would. How was she supposed to live in close proximity
to him and pretend to be his wife, while at the same time
totally resisting his attraction? Piece by piece, hour by
hour, he was contriving to weaken her will power and
destroy her defences. Alexa's scornful words about her
twin's lack of sexual experience had also left their mark
on Alissa, making her feel foolish, outdated and ignorant.
Perhaps it was true that she was guilty of making sex too
much of a big deal, she reasoned uncertainly.

Unaware of the mental moral tussle his bride was
engaged in, Sergei was now in an excellent mood while
he mentally ticked off boxes with a great deal of satisfaction. Most importantly of all, Alissa had hit it off with
Yelena. Strangely, he acknowledged, Alissa seemed to
bear no resemblance to the woman described in the psychological profile he had had done on her. How was that
possible? Did it mean that such profiles could be so in-
accurate that they were not worth the paper they were
written on? Or was it simply that Alissa was an excellent actress, well up to the challenge of concealing her
less engaging traits of character?

But why on earth was he splitting hairs when she was
putting on a wonderful performance? Evidently he had
picked the right woman for the role and now all he had
to do was get her pregnant. Not a challenge he was
likely to shrink from, he conceded with dark sexual
amusement. The arousal that always assailed him to
some degree in Alissa's presence was already charging
his lean powerful body with erotic expectancy.

Outside the hotel doors being spread wide for their
entrance, Sergei scooped Alissa up into his arms and
carried her over the threshold to the accompaniment of

the shouts, cheers and comments freely offered by the guests grouped in the foyer. Perhaps that was the first hint that Alissa received that Russian weddings were often a good deal less sedate than English ones. Everything seemed rather more colourful and informal.

As soon as they were seated a man stood up to toast the newly-weds and moments later there was an outcry of, *'Gorko! Gorko!'*

'Now we kiss for as long as we can,' Sergei told her, brilliant dark eyes frowning at her bewildered expression. 'Didn't you bother to read the information you were sent?'

Alexa had struck again, Alissa recognised in frustration, and annoyance filled her. That was the moment that Sergei chose to pry her lips apart with the tender pressure of his slow, sensual mouth. That more subtle approach wasn't what she expected from him and ironically she initially tensed in surprise. But when he dipped his tongue between her lips, her knees developed a responsive wobble and her hands crept up round his neck to steady herself. The guests were chanting but she didn't know what they were saying. Indeed the presence of an audience could only be a source of discomfort when Sergei was making love to her mouth with a sweet shattering eroticism that made mincemeat of her resistance. It seemed a very long time later when he finally freed her and she dropped back down into her seat dizzily, still drunk on the hot hungry taste of him and the thrumming of her awakened body.

Only a moment later when she was studying the assembled guests she was astonished to realise that she actually knew one of them. Her brightening eyes dimmed, however, when she failed to pick out the man's wife at the same table. Without a word she got up and went over to speak to him.

Crown Prince Jasim was already rising to greet her approach with a wide smile of welcome. 'Alissa, what a great pleasure it is to be at your wedding. When the invitation arrived, I'm afraid I paid no attention to the bride's identity, for it never occurred to me that I might already know her.'

'Elinor isn't here with you?' Alissa queried just as Sergei drew level and curved an arm to her slender spine.

'Sergei...' The handsome heir to the hereditary desert throne of Quaram delivered his congratulations before turning back to Alissa to answer her question about her friend and former flatmate. 'Sami has a bad dose of chickenpox and Elinor could not bring herself to leave him.'

Alissa fully understood that maternal decision on her friend's part. 'Of course, she couldn't. If Sami's miserable he'll need his mother for comfort.' She asked after Jasim and Elinor's little daughter, Mariyah. When Alissa had last seen the royal children, Mariyah had been a newborn baby.

'How did you get to know Jasim's wife?' Sergei asked, amazed that such an association had escaped his knowledge.

'I met her when she was pregnant with Sami and living in London. I was a student then and Elinor and I, along with another girl, shared a flat for a while,' she explained. 'But it's been months since I last heard from Elinor. We always meet up when she visits London. She's still one of my closest friends but since she married Jasim she's become incredibly busy. I must phone her and catch up. What's your connection with Jasim?'

'We see each other regularly at OPEC meetings. I've never met his wife but I've heard that she's a beauty.'

A warm smile lit up Alissa's heart-shaped face. 'She is. And I learned to knit purely for Sami's benefit. He was the most gorgeous baby,' she told him softly.

Someone else was toasting them and the same chant of *'Gorko! Gorko!'* started up again. Dark eyes locked appreciatively to her smiling face, Sergei took her into his arms to kiss and she was more than ready for the experience the second time around. It was like falling from an exhilarating height and burning up in the process. In the aftermath, her pulses were racing. When the wedding breakfast was served, she drank champagne and picked without much appetite at the first course she was served while an internationally famous singer took to the floor to entertain them.

In a party atmosphere that ensured that there was a good deal more drinking than eating going on, Alissa enjoyed several drinks and felt a little dizzy when she got up to dance with Sergei. She was wondering how a man she barely knew could have such a massive impact on her. Around him her body had a life of its own. She was short of breath without running and when he drew her close and the evocative scent of his skin and the cologne he used assailed her, butterflies went mad in her tummy. Inwardly she was already regretting that, with vodka flowing like literal water, she might have accepted too many of the drinks pressed on her.

'Tell me,' Alissa asked as she ditched her usual

caution while they danced, 'was a wish to please your grandmother the reason you wanted a wife?'

Sergei tensed and glanced down at her with cool dark eyes.

Alissa tilted her chin. 'There's no need to look at me as if I'm about to run off and tell the newspapers!'

His aggressive jaw line clenched. 'You had better not,' he murmured with chilling bite. 'I will not have Yelena hurt.'

'I wouldn't hurt her. She's so happy you've got married,' Alissa whispered, noting the old lady's animation as she chatted to her companions at the table. After a bad first marriage, Sergei had been understandably reluctant to take the plunge a second time. That made perfect sense to her. His caring so much for an elderly relative, however, touched her heart and showed her another side to his tough character. But her smooth brow furrowed because she could only consider his solution to Yelena's desire for him to remarry downright quixotic and blind in the short term. Surely his grandmother would only be more upset when his second marriage broke down as well?

'To ensure that you don't cause a scene, *milaya moya*,' Sergei murmured lazily, 'I will warn you that you are about to be snatched away from me. It's a tradition. I ransom you back.'

So, Alissa made no protest at being hustled out of the function room by a noisy crowd of well-refreshed guests and thrust into what she at first took for a cupboard but which, on lengthier scrutiny, she realised was a housekeeper's storage room. She leant back against the shelves and wondered how long it would take for him to pay the ransom.

Only minutes later she had her answer when the door flew open framing Sergei's tall, powerful frame. He snatched her into his arms again and kissed her, all the raw energy and white hot sexuality of his temperament poured into that potent sensual assault. As he whirled her away to a chorus of approval someone trod on her dress and she heard a worrying ripping sound.

'My dress is torn!' she exclaimed, her hands clutching the sparkling fabric over her thighs in dismay.

Sergei crouched down to examine the frayed remnant of fabric now trailing. He leapt up again and signalled someone. Ten minutes later she was standing in the bedroom of a fabulous hotel suite, clad only in her lingerie while her dress was carefully repaired in the reception room next door. She flinched and spun round in dismay when the door opened without even the hint of a warning knock.

Sergei focused on her small slender figure and the laughing comment he had meant to make fell from his memory there and then. She whipped her arms protectively round her scantily clad body but not before he had had the opportunity to enjoy an enchanting glimpse of her pale rounded curves. He leant back against the door and snapped home the lock, his dark eyes flashing hot gold at the sight of the pouting breasts encased in white gossamer-fine lace that revealed her delicate pink nipples. Her tiny waist, the feminine swell of her hips and the elegant sweep of her slender thighs only heightened his interest.

'Why are you hiding yourself? Let me see you properly, *milaya moya*,' Sergei urged, discovering to his amazement that he was as eager as a boy to see her naked. The pulse at his groin, which had kept him simmering on the edge of full arousal for hours, accelerated.

Her aquamarine eyes widened, her body quickening with a desire she couldn't stifle. His heated look of masculine appreciation flattered her, making her unexpectedly proud of her body. But innate common sense told her that such a thought was brazen and likely to get her into trouble. Furthermore she could not credit that her rather ordinary shape could compare to that of the international selection of well-known beauties he was accustomed to being with. Embarrassment and discomfiture attacked her then in a blinding wave. She sat down at the foot of the bed and crossed her arms, concealing her lightly clad body as best she could.

Sergei had had more than enough of waiting. Ever since the first night with her at his club, he had been ablaze with fierce sexual need and impatience. For a man with no concept of female reluctance or of pleasure deferred, that wait had proved a tough and thankless challenge. Now, with his lean muscular body honed to a raw edge of desire by the kissing, the dancing and the lack of privacy that had enforced rigorous restraint on his strong libido, he was intensely hungry for her and in no mood to hide it. In a sudden movement, he pitched off his jacket and yanked loose his tie.

'What on earth are you doing?' Alissa asked, wide-eyed.

'You're not very good at following through on orders, are you?' Sergei murmured in his deep, dark, accented drawl. 'That wilful independent streak is something we can work on together—'

'We can't…er…get involved,' Alissa protested, her

voice taking on a slightly shrill note that carried a hint of panic.

'There's no point in saying that we can't do what we've *already* done,' Sergei countered with fierce conviction and he reached for her hands to tug her up off the bed without further ado. 'I've been involved from the first moment I saw you. It's not what I planned; it's definitely not what I wanted. I never mix business with pleasure—'

'This *is* business,' she reminded him shakily, having discovered that those scorching golden eyes of his had sufficient impact to hold her as securely still as handcuffs and leg irons. She wanted to pull back and stay connected to him at one and the same time.

'But it's also an exception because it embraces you and I want you more than I've wanted any woman in a very long time,' Sergei imparted with charged urgency.

'You're only trying to justify yourself,' Alissa reasoned in growing desperation.

'Of course I am, *dorogaya moya*,' he responded with immense assurance. 'I've made my fortune from being a very adaptable man. We are together for the fore-seeable future and will be living in the most intimate of connections—what is logical and reasonable should guide our behaviour.'

As his masculine gaze flamed over her Alissa snatched in a sharp breath, for his keen appraisal was making her feel as self-conscious as if she were already naked. And she saw no logic whatsoever in being wildly attracted to a guy so far removed from her in terms of wealth and status. Indeed, she saw only disaster. 'It would just complicate things,' she muttered in feverish rebuttal.

Sergei knew women. She couldn't stop staring at

him, Her pupils were dilated, her lips moistly parted, her breathing audible. He could sense how close he was to victory. 'I don't do complicated. Trust me I'll keep it straightforward.'

Confident as ever, he lowered his handsome dark head, his luxuriant black hair gleaming in the light of the lamp she had lit to chase the wintry darkness of late afternoon. He pressed a teasing kiss to the corner of her tremulous lips. Instantly, revealingly, she turned her head straight into the kiss, lips parting in readiness for the exhilarating plunge o his tongue. Low in her throat she moaned when he gave her what she longed for in that first kiss and a knot of gathering sexual tension clenched tight in her pelvis, leaving her awesomely aware of her body.

How could she possibly trust him? He was notorious with women. If a supermodel or a famous actress couldn't hold him for longer than five minutes, what hope had she? But his unashamed single-minded desire for her excited Alissa and ensured that she felt truly feminine and attractive for the first time in her life. Even so she was uneasily conscious of her inexperience and suspected that it might shock him, possibly even repulse him. He shifted against her, one hand cupping her hips to tilt her to him so that she could feel the urgent vigour of the erection tenting the fine fabric of his trousers. A quiver of pure hunger, as sharp as it was painful in its intensity, slivered through her.

Sergei unclipped the bra with one hand and drew it down her arms before succumbing to the temptation of looking at her beautifully formed breasts. He cupped the pert mounds in reverent fingers. 'You are a work of art.'

His fingers brushed the lush pouting buds that crowned the full swells. He was already as hard as steel and he vented an earthy groan of appreciation and backed her down on the bed, his mouth swooping down to capture a quivering nipple to tease it with the slick of his tongue and the edge of his teeth.

That sweet torment of sensation arrowed straight down to the hot damp place between her thighs and raised her temperature to a tingling height. Her hips squirmed in a rhythm as old as time. She dragged him up to kiss her again, rejoicing in his passion but desperately hungry for more. Her untried body was soaking up every new sensation like a sponge and responding with increasing demands.

The level of her response astounded Sergei. He reeled back from her to haul at his shirt and she leant over him, tugging frantically at buttons with an eager lack of sophistication and dexterity that he found tremendously attractive.

The shirt finally conquered with the loss of only one button, Alissa studied his golden-toned torso and the pelt of curling black hair accentuating his pectoral muscles and felt weak with longing. She let her hands run unsteadily down over his stomach, felt his taut muscles contract in reaction and pressed her lips to a masculine nipple, headily drinking in the familiar smell of his skin.

'*Yizihkom,*' he breathed thickly.

'In English?' Alissa gasped.

Sergei tipped up her chin, dark golden eyes smouldering with sexual heat. 'Use your tongue,' he translated thickly, wondering at her tentative caresses and the way in which his advice caused immediate hot colour to rise in her cheeks.

Knowing she needed all the help she could get, Alissa obliged, keen to please him as much as he had pleased her and driven on by the fire of craving at the heart of her. He tasted every bit as good as he looked and had he not pushed her back onto the mattress to torment the hard buds of her sensitised nipples, she would certainly have become more daring. Her downfall was complete when he employed a seeking hand below the lace panties and found the precise spot to tease, destroying what remained of her self control. With a helpless cry she arched up to him and he crushed her mouth below his, his tongue meshing with hers in an erotic dance.

'Please...oh, *please*!' Alissa moaned, burning with all-encompassing need and beyond thought.

With a roughened curse half under his breath, Sergei ripped off her panties and discovered the warm wet welcome awaiting him with a savage sound of overpoweringly male satisfaction. Springing upright, he dispensed with his own clothing while she looked up at him with dazed eyes of need.

He was so beautiful—a pagan vision of bronzed muscular power and energy. He was also very aroused and her first sight of a fully erect male was daunting.

'We'll never fit!' she told him before she could think better of it.

Sergei laughed out loud, for it struck him as such a naïve and irrational comment from a woman who had stated in an interview that she considered herself very much a woman of the world and comfortable with men.

'I am so hot for you, I am in pain,' he confessed, coming down to her again.

He entered her hard and fast and she yelped and flinched with pain.

An incredulous look in his hot golden gaze, as he had felt the resistance of her flesh to his invasion, he growled, 'You cannot be a virgin…'

'Why? Is there a law against it?' Alissa countered, her low voice raw with embarrassment and the lingering shards of discomfort still throbbing through her tender flesh.

'Do you want me to stop?' Sergei was frozen with frustration and a hunger that made him tremble because the lush, tight fit of her tiny body round him was extraordinarily pleasurable.

He was already trying and failing to replace the image of the woman he had thought she was with the woman she now appeared to be. He had picked a wife he'd believed would spring no surprises on him. Better the devil you know, he had decided, and who had more experience than he of shallow, unemotional and mercenary women? Instead he had found himself a virgin and suddenly he understood the blushes and the awkwardness and the confusing signals she gave him. He studied her from below the screen of his ink-black lashes and the rarity of the gift she had given him finally struck him. She was his wife and no one but him had ever got this intimate with her. It was a thought that had strong appeal for a male as discerning as he was. The disturbing surprise suddenly became a cause for celebration.

'Don't stop,' she breathed, helpless in the grip of the erotic heat and intensity still roaring through her.

Expelling his breath in a hiss of relief, Sergei began to move again while exerting every atom of control that he could muster. He responded well to challenge and he was determined to exceed whatever expectations she had of the event. His fluid increase in tempo sent excitement flashing through Alissa faster than an express train and fuelled her need. She bucked under him and sobbed with startled pleasure when he employed slow subtle movements that tormented her with sensation. She couldn't control anything that she was feeling and what she was feeling was incredibly powerful. The hunger stoked by his passion reached a frantic height when every part of her was pitched to an unbearable degree of longing and then in a breathless heartbeat she reached an ecstatic climax. As she writhed under him in frenzied abandonment, wave after wave of pleasure convulsing her slender body, Sergei enjoyed the longest and most stupendous release of his life. His superb body shuddering over her, he tasted the ecstasy.

A split second later, he was wondering with an amount of alarm that shook him whether that single act of stunning sex might get her pregnant. And he didn't want her carrying a child too soon, did he? Momentarily, Sergei, who never, ever deviated from a goal once he was set on it, was plunged into genuine bewilderment by his own change of heart on the baby issue. But when she conceived, it would surely be a case of game over as far as the bedroom was concerned and he really did not want to put her out of commission in the first month. That said, however, his priorities were unchanged, he reassured himself confidently: he was simply taking a rain check on that objective. Why shouldn't he want to enjoy his bride for a while? There wasn't a man alive who would not want to make the most of a woman who gave him that much pleasure between the sheets, he reasoned, his tension ebbing again. Releasing her from his weight, he anchored her to him with an appreciative arm.

'*Bihla chudyesna*…that was amazing,' he told her with husky satisfaction, landing a haphazard kiss on her cheekbone and then backing off so fast in discomfiture at having given her that salutation that she almost fell off the bed. 'But we have a reception to get back to.'

Shot back to reality with a vengeance by that reminder, Alissa slid off the bed as if she had been jabbed by a hot poker. Realising in mortification that, aside of a wispy bra and a pair of torn knickers, she had no clothes to put back on, she snatched at the bedspread and yanked violently at it to haul it from under the big bronzed length of him where he lay in an infuriatingly relaxed post-coital sprawl. Concealing herself within its folds, Alissa was furiously aware of Sergei's unashamedly amused scrutiny.

'What is hidden is always more intriguing, *angil moy*,' he murmured with silken approbation. 'And much more appealing to a man like me than a short skirt and a low neckline—'

'Intriguing you is the very last thing on my mind!' Alissa almost spat at him, a tempestuous fury building behind her embarrassment.

With his brilliant dark eyes gleaming, his black hair ruffled and blue-black stubble beginning to shadow his strong jaw line and highlight his shapely mouth, he was a pagan vision of male beauty and magnetism. And she hated him, absolutely hated him for taking advantage of

her the very first chance he got! Or the very first chance
she had *given* him, she rephrased bitterly, loathing
herself even more than she loathed him. But then what
else had she expected from Sergei Antonovich? He was
programmed to take advantage. He was a billionaire
buccaneer in business, famous for his unpredictability
and ability to move fast on a choice deal.

'How much did I hurt you?' he enquired with lazy
assurance.

Her face burned. 'I'm not going to discuss that—I'm
not going to discuss anything that happened in that bed
because there's no need. It's never going to happen again!'

Sergei was happily engaged in admiring the way the
silk spread poured over her ripe little curves to cradle a
pouting breast and define a deliciously voluptuous
buttock. That green shade threw her aquamarine eyes
into prominence as well. He was hugely relieved to hear
that she didn't want to discuss anything. Particularly
anything that related to how their business contract had
suddenly expanded to include sex for pleasure.

Unusually for him, he wasn't quite sure why the
business angle was taking more and more of a back
seat, but he suspected it had a lot to do with the reality
that he had wanted to bed her from the first instant he
laid eyes on her tiny curvy frame. Why should that be
a problem? She was proving to be a very worthwhile in-
vestment and there was no reason why he shouldn't
keep her as an indulgence for as long as he wanted. By
the time she had given him a baby, she would no longer
be a novelty, he reckoned with cynical conviction. An
awareness of his own notorious track record warned
him that familiarity would soon breed, not only con-

tempt, but also boredom, and he would be glad to see her go.

'You took advantage of the fact that I had had too much to drink!' Alissa launched her attack without warning.

'Had you?' His black brows drew together. 'When you were ripping off my shirt you struck me as an equal partner in every respect,' he mused with the aura of a male recalling that act with satisfaction. 'Don't spoil it by being childish.'

'Childish?' Alissa parroted in a rage.

'Why does the timing matter?' he demanded in sincere incomprehension, for he had baulked at the prospect of a child conceived by artificial means in a Petri dish and sex had always been part of the package deal. 'We wanted each other and we went to bed—'

'We didn't even make it *into* the bed!' Alissa snapped accusingly, wondering why he was talking about timing, since she could not see what that had to do with anything.

An almost imperceptible darkening of colour high-lighted Sergei's high cheekbones. He was willing to admit that as encounters went it might not have been the idealis-tic stuff of a virginal fantasy. But then, he was well aware that she was not a romantic woman. No romantic woman would accept a huge amount of money to marry a stranger, give him a child and then walk away from that child.

'It's too late for regrets,' Sergei pointed out with innate practicality.

Outraged by his attitude, Alissa stalked into the en-suite bathroom to stare shell-shocked at herself in the mirror above the vanity unit. Her wreath of flowers was crushed, her veil creased and her make-up smeared all over her face. She looked like a car-crash bride and the illusion of perfection was long gone. Tear tracks streaked her face while she stood there recognising that she had just totally changed her relationship with Sergei. Sex had smashed the boundaries she had known she had to retain if she was ever to win his respect. Her body ached with her every movement. She showered as best she could without getting her hair wet.

A knock made the door bounce in its frame and she spun round and opened it a mere crack, because she knew exactly who had to be behind that too-powerful knock.

'I'm going for a shower in the other bedroom.'

Consternation made Alissa open the door wider and note the fact that he was only wearing his trousers with his shirt hanging open. 'For goodness' sake, put on all your clothes before you step out of this room!'

'Why?'

Her mouth snapped into a compressed line at what she saw as a very stupid question. 'Because if you don't the women out there fixing my dress will realise exactly what we've been doing!'

'*So?*' Sergei prompted very drily, thinking not for the first time that Alissa's attitudes and declarations frequently defied all logic and reality. 'We got married, we shagged, so far, so normal…'

Alissa breathed in so deep she was afraid that she would burn up with the internal heat of her vexation. 'If you don't put your clothes on, I'll never forgive you!' she snapped in dire warning.

'They'll know anyway,' Sergei told her with impatience. 'You've wrecked your hair and the flowers in the wreath, so I asked the beautician and the florist to come up and sort you out.'

Scarlet to her hairline, Alissa gave him what could only be described as a very aggressive and freezing nod, before shutting the door in his lean, darkly handsome face. Later she could never work out quite how she managed to handle the reappearance of the support team, entrusted with licking her back into bridal shape, because inside herself she was cringing. The knowing looks when she reappeared at the reception by Sergei's side ate her alive with mortification. His reputation went before him, she reflected ruefully. When Sergei disappeared with a woman, no one, it seemed, had any doubt of his intent.

Intercepting a warm smile from Yelena, Alissa went over to talk as best she could to Sergei's grandmother. The grizzled bearded man by her side revealed that he was a retired professor living in Yelena's village and he translated to enable the two women to communicate. Alissa was surprised to find that she was confiding in Yelena about her parents' separation.

Sergei joined them and spoke at length to his grandmother before closing a hand over Alissa's and guiding her onto the dance floor. She glanced up at his lean, breathtakingly handsome face and her heart thumped heavily in her eardrums. She felt so vulnerable, so unsure of what to do next, for the passion they had shared had wrecked the framework of their relationship and she had no idea what would replace it.

'We're leaving,' Sergei explained only when she questioned why they were leaving the function room and by a side door. 'Yelena's right. You look exhausted... like a little white ghost, *angil moy*...'

CHAPTER SIX

PINK colour swam up below Alissa's fair skin in a revealing tide.

In the limo, Sergei slid a long brown forefinger below her chin to tip up her face. 'You're still angry with me,' he noted in apparent surprise.

'No, I'm not. I'm not a child either. I do appreciate that I was equally responsible for what occurred,' she said woodenly, long feathery lashes veiling her aquamarine eyes from his scrutiny.

Unholy amusement lit up Sergei's smile; he was in an unusually good mood. She was still furious with him and couldn't hide it and he loved that transparency of hers for its rarity. Her refusal to meet his eyes and her rigidity spoke for her. Women didn't treat him that way and her nerve in doing so intrigued him. She was a novelty and so far the exact opposite of the woman described in that psychological profile. She was warm when she was supposed to be cool, passionate when she was supposed to be indifferent and deeply attached to her family when she was supposed to be selfish and detached. Even so, whatever conundrum Alissa presented, she had put on a marvellous show for his grand-mother's benefit.

'I have a gift for you.' Sergei presented her with a jewel case.

'Another one?' Alissa asked in disbelief and she was annoyed when that tart response only made her feel rude and ungracious.

'I always reward excellence and you surpassed my highest expectations today,' Sergei drawled as smooth as glass.

'At the wedding…or on the bed?' Alissa queried in a frozen little voice of supreme scorn.

Her tone was wasted on Sergei, who merely vented an appreciative laugh that emphasised how far apart they were in terms of humour. 'You were a triumph everywhere, *angil moy.*'

With pronounced reluctance Alissa flipped up the lid of the case to reveal a diamond necklace that would surely have been worthy of the Crown jewels exhibited in the Tower of London. In spite of the fact that she was determined not to be impressed, her lips fell wide as she gazed at the river of perfectly matched glittering stones embellished by a magnificent pendant with a huge opulent emerald at its heart.

'Well, thank you very much,' she muttered finally, re-minding herself that Alexa would have snatched it up, put it on and wrapped her arms gratefully round his neck in reward for such generosity.

'Don't you like jewellery?'

'Oh, very much,' she hastened to declare, steeling herself to remove the necklace from the case and behave as he almost certainly expected her to and wrap it straight round her neck. 'But you really don't need to give me stuff like this.'

Sergei did up the clasp. The stunning pendant was heavy and cold on her skin. *Her reward for excellence.* Alissa remembered that wild raunchy coupling on the bed, which had evidently pleased him very much. Her tummy clenched with a disturbing combination of intense shame and equally intense excitement. Her virginity hadn't repulsed him in the slightest and, although what she had allowed to happen between them felt indisputably wrong and her pride lay in ashes round her feet, Sergei *still* didn't repulse her. What was the matter with her? Where had her values gone?

The limousine wafted them back to his imposing city residence. He took her hand in the hall and directed her up the sweeping staircase.

'Where are we going?' she queried when he walked her past the room she had slept in the night before.

'Your new room.'

'Is it your room as well?' Alissa enquired tightly.

'No, I'm not into that joined-at-the-hip cosy couple stuff,' Sergei imparted with perceptible recoil at the idea. 'Not my style. I have my own suite next door.'

Alissa's tension eased at the news that she was not expected to share a room with him. Surely with that sensible demarcation line in place there was less chance that she would be tempted by him again?

Sergei opened the door. He escorted her across the depth of a superb large bedroom and paused on the threshold of the en suite where odd flickering shadows were lighting up the walls. Alissa moved past him to gape in astonishment at the sunken bath already filled with steaming water and encircled with candles.

Sergei rested both hands on her narrow shoulders. 'This has been a stressful day for you but you rose wonderfully to the challenge. I want you to relax now.' He flipped her gently round, detached the wreath and veil, cast them carelessly aside and began without hesitation to unfasten her dress.

'I can manage fine without help!' Alissa exclaimed.

'I don't think so.' Sergei breathed in the warm and already familiar scent of her. She smelled of the perfume he had bought her in London, a light but lingering floral fragrance that suited her so much better than the more exotic cloying concoction she had sported at their first meeting. He pressed his sensual masculine mouth against the soft skin of the fine-boned shoulder he had bared, his lips moving in a caressing trail to her sensitive nape while he slowly eased the fitted sleeves down her arms. Alissa quivered in response as though he were touching much more intimate places. Never ever had she dreamt that it was possible to be so insanely aware of a man. As her knees threatened to buckle and her stress level rose like steam in a tightly lidded pot she fought her treacherous weakness with all her might. And then suddenly without warning it was all too much for her and she sagged back into the shelter of his strong arms, tears burning the backs of her troubled eyes.

'Don't do that,' she told him shakily.

'But you like what I do to you,' Sergei asserted with husky assurance, sliding his hands below the loosened bodice to nudge her lace bra out of his path and cup the soft silken mounds of her breasts in his palms. Her nipples tightened into tingling erection below the skilled stroke of his thumbs.

'Whether I like it or not is irrelevant!' Alissa argued wildly.

'How can it be?' Sergei urged, turning her round to face him. 'It's the icing on the cake for both of us. But you should have warned me that I would be your first lover. If I'd known I would have been more patient and I might have hurt you less.'

Alissa wanted the tiled floor to open up and swallow her. She snatched at her bodice before it could tumble lower and expose her bare breasts. Her hands were trembling, for she was remembering that wild passion when his impatience had only been matched by her eagerness and the pain had drowned in the hot sweet tide of pleasure. Her face burning, she stepped back from him. 'I'm fine,' she said flatly.

Sergei dealt her a flashing smile of such intrinsic charisma that her gaze stayed glued to him. 'We'll eat together in an hour.'

Relieved by his departure and wrung out by the day's events, Alissa shed her dress in the bedroom and finally sank into the bath with a heartfelt sigh of pleasure. Rose petals floated on the surface of the fragrant water. Sergei, she acknowledged in wonderment, had actually pre-arranged the candlelit bath for her and she was impressed, much more impressed than she had been by the gift of the extravagant diamond and emerald necklace. She shifted position and the dulled throb of her still tender flesh mocked her. So she was fine, was she?

She had had a lust-fuelled sexual encounter for the very first time and, while she was still ashamed of herself, she was even more worried that it would take very little effort on his part to persuade her into a repetition. The whole situation ran against her every principle and just then she could not work out how she had got caught up in it. She was his wife, his bought and paid for wife, who had already agreed to let him go without a fuss when he wanted his freedom back. He saw no reason why they shouldn't make the most of the attraction between them in the meantime. Alexa would probably have laughed and settled for a short-lived casual affair, Alissa reflected uncomfortably. Why did she want more from Sergei than that fleeting sexual interest?

What did she like about Sergei Antonovich? It amazed her that she had disliked him so thoroughly at their first meeting. But then she had learned more about him since then, she reasoned.

He was very fond of his grandmother and so determined to make the older woman happy that he was willing to fake a marriage for her benefit. Alissa believed that he had made the wrong decision on that score, but she couldn't fault his good intentions. She also liked the fact that for all his wealth and power he didn't take himself too seriously. And his manners were faultless. He opened doors, held out coats for her, asked if she was cold and generally practised the kind of courtesy that had fallen out of fashion with so many men. He made her feel incredibly feminine as well. And although he was extremely blunt she preferred honesty to hypocrisy and evasion. Besides, while he was indisputably arrogant and bossy, he could also be surprisingly thoughtful and considerate, she conceded, resting back in the sunken tub with a dreamy smile blossoming on her face. When a maid rapped on the door to deliver a box of handmade chocolates to the very side of the bath, Alissa's smile shone even brighter. She let a chocolate melt against her taste buds and sighed in bliss while she allowed her thoughts to drift for long timeless moments.

I really really fancy him. I want to sleep with him tonight. I'm falling in love with him like some silly infatuated schoolgirl!

Eyes wide with shock and dismay at the thoughts suddenly chasing without warning through her bemused head, Alissa sat up with a start, water sloshing noisily around her. Conscious that the water was cooling by then, she got out of the bath and wrapped her slender figure in a white fleecy towel. Only taking the time to remove her make-up and comb her hair, she returned to the bedroom just as the phone by the bed buzzed.

'Come and join me,' Sergei urged lazily. 'I've just had to sack the manager of my football team!'

Alissa rummaged through the drawers in the dressing room for nightwear. Everything had been unpacked and neatly put away for her. Sliding into a turquoise nightdress in haste, she pulled on the matching wrap while chanting a firm mantra to herself. I am not going to have sex with him again. *I am not going to have sex with him again under any circumstances. We're just going to talk about football. But I do hope I don't have to watch any.*

Sergei, his lean, beautifully built body clad solely in a pair of black silk designer boxers, was pacing the floor of the room next door and talking on the phone in a foreign language. He was also gesticulating with a good deal of force to express his feelings. With the fingers of one brown hand he indicated the trolley of food by the bed in an invitation for her to help herself.

Alissa only then realised that she was actually rave-nously hungry and she lifted a plate and selected choice morsels of food from the sizeable assortment of hot and cold dishes on offer. Forcing her attention away from the clothes discarded untidily on the carpet, she curled up on the bed and munched happily through a selection of chicken, salad and fresh baked bread. Sergei com-pleted his phone call, treated her to a spirited speech about unreliable temperamental staff and embarked straight away on another phone call. She didn't quite grasp what all the fuss was about and truthfully didn't much care. Halfway through her own meal she set it aside and filled a plate for him, placing it where he could reach it while he paced back and forth.

'How many languages do you speak?' she enquired between calls.

'Six or seven and enough to make myself understood in basic terms in another couple,' he breathed as if the talent were nothing unusual. 'When I do business, I like to be able to talk to people direct rather than through intermediaries.'

'I speak French and Spanish but not fluently,' she told him modestly.

'You have to learn Russian,' he replied.

'Do I?'

His black brows drew together in a frown at the question. 'Of course, *milaya moya*.'

Sergei studied her, striving to dissect the precise source of her ever-growing appeal because, just at that moment, she looked more like a teenager than an adult.

Her face shone with cleanliness and her hair was tucked untidily behind her ears. Natural and unadorned, she bore no resemblance to the high maintenance women who normally shared his bed. She had beautiful eyes though, very clear and expressive. They were by far her best feature, although that soft, full-lipped mouth was worthy of note too, he conceded, while at the same time noting the fine smooth grain of her skin and the appealing delicacy of her bone structure. His appetite for food dwindled to be replaced by another kind of hunger while he appraised her and recalled more intimate images that sent the blood pounding through his veins.

Struggling to appear unaware of that lengthy all-male scrutiny, Alissa asked herself what she was doing sitting on his bed. Was that being standoffish? More businesslike in her approach? Discouraging? Shame sat like a lump of lead in her stomach but she didn't budge. Without warning the prospect of keeping her distance from him and restoring platonic limits had all the appeal of a heavy rainstorm on her horizon.

'I like that you're completely sober,' Sergei commented.

'I learned to leave my glass full and everyone stopped pushing more drinks in my direction,' she confided with a comical expression.

Charmed by that cheeky smile, Sergei switched off his phone, tossed it aside and reached for her with purposeful hands. She came up on her knees and he knotted one hand in the heavy fall of her golden hair and slowly, sexily ravished her mouth while he pushed the wrap and the straps of her nightie down off her slim shoulders. As the garments fell to her knees he captured her breasts and kneaded the quivering tips until she was gasping, shaken by the immediate surge of heat between her thighs.

'I can't stop wanting you,' Sergei growled, long fingers dropping down to part the golden curls on her mound and gently tease the sensitive bud of her clitoris before venturing to stroke the lush damp lips she would have hidden from him.

Her breath was rattling in her tight throat. She parted her thighs for him, awkwardly balancing herself with a hand on his shoulder until he hauled her up into his arms and tipped her back on the bed. Her body was humming, as desperate for every caress as though their earlier encounter had never happened. He kissed a tormenting passage down over her writhing, shifting length.

'I want to make love to you the way I should have this afternoon,' Sergei breathed thickly. 'I can't wait to drive you crazy with pleasure.'

And just as he knew what he was doing, she did as well. Later she would make herself acknowledge that shameful fact, but while he was doing gloriously arousing things to her weak and easily tempted body she was a complete pushover. What she was feeling was impossibly strong and left no room for questions of right and wrong. He pleasured her with his mouth and his tongue and his fingers until she was a trembling, overheated heap of excited nerve-endings crying out for more.

Hot and ready, she watched him as he donned protection. When he finally sank into the tight wet sheath of her womanhood, the sheer excitement of his entrance sent her careening headlong into violent orgasm. Her sobs and convulsions of delight almost made Sergei lose control as well. Fierce strain etched in the hard, handsome contours of his face, he lifted her knees to hold her still and drove his hard male heat into her yielding flesh with insistent hunger.

Her excitement never once dropped by so much as an atom and she soon hit another high, a climax ripping through her like fireworks blazing up. Afterwards she thought she would never move again. Her limbs were heavy, her body languorous and the most amazing sense of well-being and peace engulfed her. Sergei rolled over, keeping his arms wrapped round her so that he carried her with him.

'You are so hot, *angil moy*,' he intoned, his stunning dark golden eyes glittering with rich appreciation, his heart still thundering against her, his bronzed length damp with sweat. 'I may never let you get out of this bed again.'

Alissa was so exhausted that she had no strength left to move. She consoled herself by dabbing kisses on whichever part of him she could reach and he stretched indolently and this time around he stayed close, letting her have her way.

'Yelena told me you're still stressing about the breakdown of your parents' marriage,' Sergei murmured. 'That's crazy—'

Alissa stiffened. 'Why is it crazy?'

'You lived in a happy united family for over twenty years. You should appreciate how lucky you were.'

Alissa blinked in shock at that rebuke from an unexpected quarter. 'Why? What was your experience?' she snapped, mortified by his criticism.

'A father in and out of prison for stealing cars—he

was a thief and a stupid one. I also had to put my mother to bed drunk every night,' he breathed wryly. 'My father was shot dead in the street for stealing a local gangster's car and a year later my mother's liver finally quit and she died…'

Caught up in the dark story of his childhood, Alissa wriggled round in the circle of his arms to look at him wide-eyed with disquiet. 'What age were you then?'

His lean strong face bore no emotion. He might have been talking about someone else's life. 'Thirteen. Yelena insisted on giving me a home with her. We were strangers because my father was a lousy son as well,' Sergei recounted levelly, grim dark eyes meeting hers. 'She was my only experience of family life and I gave her a hard time. I was as feral as a wild animal.'

Alissa traced the stubborn shape of his sensual lower lip with an admiring fingertip. 'I can imagine that.'

Sergei released a spontaneous laugh of disagreement. 'No, you can't. We grew up in different worlds. Yours was cosy, middle class and protected. I bet you got just about everything you ever wanted.'

'No, I didn't!'

'Tell me one thing you didn't get,' Sergei challenged, absorbed in the constant play of animation across her heart-shaped face, while he wondered why he was talking to her when he never wasted time doing that with a woman.

'I fell in love with someone else's boyfriend once,' Alissa admitted, offended by his apparent belief that she had been spoiled and cosseted with good fortune all her days. 'I had to get over it, but it was a very unhappy time for me.'

'Didn't you make a play for him?'

Alissa gave him a shocked look. 'Of course not. He was my sister's boyfriend.'

'If you weren't prepared to fight for him, you can't have wanted him that much, *milaya moya*,' Sergei quipped, wondering darkly if she would fight for him or whether she was guilty of being as shallow as her profile beneath that surface show of niceness.

'Sergei...' she said ruefully. 'There are such things as family loyalty and moral standards.'

'I wonder if our child will inherit your outlook.' His dark brows drew together in a slight grimace. 'I'm very cold-blooded when it comes to protecting my own interests. One or two of your genes mightn't do too much damage but too many would make him or her weak in my world.'

In receipt of that speech, Alissa blinked in bewilderment and jerked back from him. '*Our child?* What are you talking about?'

Scanning her perplexed face with a frown, Sergei loosened his hold on her, allowing her to break the connection. 'If that's a joke, it's not a very good one.'

'Why would it be a joke? I agreed to marry you...'

'And have my baby, as you are very well aware,' Sergei countered with impatience. 'But if you agree, and I don't see why you shouldn't, I'm willing to push the time frame back a month or two.'

And have my baby. That fatal assurance rang like a clarion call in Alissa's head and froze her to the marrow. Alexa could not possibly have agreed to such an iniquitous contract. It couldn't be true, it *couldn't* be!

CHAPTER SEVEN

'WHAT are you doing?' Sergei demanded as Alissa slid soundlessly off the side of the bed like a wraith trying to avoid detection. In almost the same movement she reached for her discarded nightdress.

Alissa's upper lip was damp with perspiration. She had broken out in a literal cold sweat. Why would Sergei lie? Nor had there been anything teasing about his voice or manner. Indeed he'd had been terrifyingly matter-of-fact when he mentioned putting back the time frame for a while. A baby? She was to give him a baby as part of the contract? He had to be out of his mind!

She pulled on her nightie with shaking hands, for the nakedness of intimacy seemed more wrong than ever now that she was being forced to confront the reality that to protect her sister she had deceived him. Was it possible that Alexa could have set out to deceive her as well? It was after midnight and Alissa was incredibly tired. There were no bright ideas in her mind to inspire her and no magical escape hatch in sight. So desperate was she to know exactly what Sergei was talking about that she felt that her only option was to come clean.

'We need to talk,' Alissa breathed tautly.

Wondering what on earth she was up to, Sergei had already sat up to view her with narrowed and intent dark eyes. 'It's late,' he responded, wishing he hadn't broken the habit of a lifetime and started sharing confidences with her. Somehow she was getting under his skin and he didn't like that.

Alissa laced her hands together. 'I'm afraid we've got to talk because when you mentioned having a baby I genuinely didn't know what you were talking about—'

'Bearing in mind the contract you signed and the legal advice you had beforehand, that's an impossible claim for you to make.' Brilliant dark eyes now glinting with cold incredulity, Sergei thrust back the bedding to spring out of bed. 'What are you trying to do to me?'

Alissa hovered while he strode into what appeared to be a dressing room similar to hers and disappeared briefly from view. She listened to doors being opened, drawers being rammed in and out with a force that defeated their smooth gliding mechanism. The tension in the air was already making her tummy queasy. The sheer scale of the deception she had engaged in was suddenly hitting her for the very first time. It seemed to her that she could only have walked blindfold into marrying him with her brain on hold. Only now, when she had to break the silence of secrecy, was she able to fully contemplate the enormity of what she had done.

Sergei emerged, sheathed in well-worn jeans and a black T-shirt. Barefoot, every inch of his long muscular physique taut, he surveyed her, his lean dark features set in forbidding lines. 'Explain yourself.'

Her heart beating very fast, Alissa breathed in deep, wondered where on earth to begin and decided to go straight to the crux of the matter. 'It was my sister who initially applied for this…er…role. She went through the whole interview procedure using my name and my educational background…'

His bronzed skin stretched taut over his proud bone structure. A hint of pallor was detracting from his healthy colour. 'Your…*sister*? Are you seriously trying to tell me that you are not the woman who was vetted to become my wife?'

The tension was so fierce that her spine was rigid. 'Yes. I know it must sound awful to you, but there was truly no malicious intent involved in the exchange.'

Taut with savage disbelief at that either excessively naïve or excessively stupid assessment of the damage done, Sergei's hands slowly coiled into fists of restraint by his side. He could not immediately credit the possibility that he could have spent a fortune recruiting the perfect wife and the future mother of his child only to end up being duped by a complete con artist and her accomplice in crime. The very idea of it enraged him. Transgressions of that nature didn't happen to Sergei. He had little experience of monumental foul-ups because he employed a large staff of the very best professionals available to protect him.

Alissa was torn between relief at his silence and terror of what he might be about to say to her. She made a slightly clumsy pleading movement with one hand and took a step forward. 'My sister, Alexa, is my twin—my identical twin.'

Comprehension hit Sergei like a punch in the stomach. He immediately recalled the sour skinny version of her in the photograph. He had got the little, smiley, curvy virgin one instead when he might well have rejected the original in the flesh. Recalling his misgivings over Alissa's failure to match his initial expectations and, even more gallingly, the background check he had cancelled out of pure lust, he cursed and only half under his breath. He should have insisted that she be checked out. He had only himself to blame on that score. Why had he let her sex appeal overrule the shrewd intelligence and preservation instincts that until now had kept him safe?

'You do realise that you and your sister have committed fraud?'

Alissa turned very pale indeed at that charge and busied her trembling hands in picking up her wrap and putting it on. *'Fraud?'* she queried unsteadily, sheer horror at the assurance that she was guilty of a crime scrambling her ability to think straight.

'Who went through the elimination process for this role?'

'Alexa.'

'For the entire process?' Sergei prompted.

Alissa nodded confirmation, her eyes full of anxiety.

'Who signed the contract?' he continued

'Alexa…in my name. She forged my signature,' Alissa told him unwillingly.

Reining back a burst of volcanic rage that would have blown her out of the room, Sergei allowed himself to wonder whether, in the light of those facts, she was still his legal wife. He levelled hard dark eyes of purpose on the bird he had in hand and knew that, impostor or otherwise, he had no intention of letting her out of his sight for longer than five minutes lest she make a run for it. Fired up by the danger of that risk, Sergei lifted the phone to speak to his security chief, Borya, and gave the older man a ream of detailed instructions. He commenced with an order for background reports on Alissa and her twin sister and concluded with the directive that his wife's phone calls be recorded and her every move watched.

Breathing in short shallow bursts, Alissa waited for Sergei to turn back to her. Fraud was a hard, scary word and she felt incredibly stupid for not having expected it to be thrown at her.

'You're an impostor,' Sergei told her with icy precision.

Alissa nibbled worriedly at her lower lip. 'Yes.'

'A liar—'

'I haven't had to tell any lies!' she protested.

'From the first night we met you've been lying to me by pretending to be your sister,' he rephrased his charge grimly. 'Why?'

Alissa had never been so conscious of his size as she was standing in that lamplit bedroom with his dark shadow falling across her. His anger was like a physical entity in the room, for the atmosphere was explosive. She breathed in deep and slow.

'While Alexa was going through the application, she started dating someone and she fell pregnant by him. So, of course, then she couldn't go through with marrying you, but she'd already spent the money you gave her—'

'What? All...' Sergei quoted a massive head-spinning amount of money and suddenly it was Alissa's turn to gape at him in disbelief. 'Even the biggest spend-thrift would find it hard to spend that much in so short a period.'

'You *can't* have given Alexa that much money!' Alissa exclaimed in astonishment.

'Don't act the innocent. You and your sister were playing for very high stakes and you got away with the cash. But pause and consider your predicament for a moment. I have never allowed anyone to get away with cheating me,' Sergei informed her softly.

A quiver of cold alarm was trickling down Alissa's tense spine while anger was beginning to spark inside her. 'There was never any intention of cheating you—'

'Then how come I paid and got an impostor and a liar who expects me to believe that she doesn't even know what was in the contract her sister signed in her name?' Sergei angled harshly at her.

'I never got the chance to see the contract!' Alissa slammed back at him defensively.

In answer, Sergei swept up the laptop on the chest near the bed and hit several buttons on the keyboard before angling it in her direction. 'Here…your recommended bedtime reading. It's the contract. If you're telling me the truth, which I doubt,' he said coldly, 'don't you think that neglecting to read what you were signing up for was very foolish?'

'But I didn't sign up for it originally…'

'Who got the cash?'

'Alexa used it to help Mum keep her home and business and pay off Dad's claim on them.'

'What a saint of a daughter!' Sergei derided. 'Are you planning to play the same violins for my benefit? Save your breath. Sob stories leave me cold.'

Clutching at the laptop, Alissa lifted her chin. 'I've none to tell you. But Alexa was totally honest. If she hadn't been pregnant she would have gone ahead and married you!'

'Try some joined-up thinking,' Sergei advised with stinging scorn.

'And what's that supposed to mean?' Alissa shot back at him.

'According to what you've told me your sister used your name from the outset in this scam,' Sergei reminded her very drily. 'Obviously there was no way that she could *ever* have planned to marry me when she was masquerading under your name! That would have been a legal impossibility.'

In receipt of that shrewd and contemptuous assurance, Alissa dealt him a fuming appraisal, infuriated by his insinuations. Just then she was in the grip of shock and it was beyond her capability to compute that fact and doubt her sister's intentions when her own actions had always been powered by family loyalty. 'You've said enough—'

Sergei flung open the communicating door to her bedroom in a blunt invitation for her to leave. 'I've only just begun.'

'What are you going to do…now that you know?' Alissa asked nervously.

'I'm not about to be the loser in this scenario,' Sergei drawled, smooth as silk. 'Be assured of that. I may well prosecute you and your sister for fraud.'

Alissa twisted her hands together. 'Sergei…nobody meant to do you any harm. It was just the way things happened and Alexa was in a complete panic—'

His lean, darkly handsome face was cold and set, his dark eyes merciless. 'If you're not prepared to fulfil that contract in her place, I've been cheated and I won't accept that. I'll tell you what I intend to do tomorrow.'

That last assurance made her blood run cold but there was one question she just had to ask. 'Did Alexa really agree to have a baby with you?' she framed unevenly.

'Not so much with me, as *for* me. Study the contract,' Sergei instructed flatly. 'You're very lucky I'm not throwing you out on the street right now! As far as I'm concerned you're a lying, cheating con artist.'

That judgement hit Alissa hard. As the door snapped shut in her face she backed over to the bed and sat down to focus on the contract on the screen. It was very long and involved and by the time she had finished rereading the more complex clauses she was ashen pale and shattered by the lies and omissions her twin had employed to lure her into taking her place.

On one very telling issue Sergei had been hatefully accurate. Alexa *had* walked away with a fantastic sum of cash, far, far more than Alissa could ever have estimated. Furthermore it would only have taken less than a quarter of that money to settle their mother's financial problems, so Alexa had enriched herself considerably by signing that contract in her sister's name.

Alissa was in deep shock and questions she had never dreamt she might ask about her sister were now tormenting her. Had Alexa planned to use Alissa as a dupe from the outset? What else was she supposed to think? Trust Sergei to pick up on the fact that, having used Alissa's name to begin with, Alexa could never have followed through on the contract she had signed.

Devastating as that possibility was, Alissa was a good deal more appalled by the actual content of the contract.

Sergei hadn't only wanted a wife to please his grandmother, he had wanted a child as well and, having spelt out those terms in advance, he was expecting the bride he had hired for the purpose to supply him with one. Where did that leave them both? She could not even countenance the idea of having a child with him, never mind giving that same child up wholly into his care. She curled up in her cold bed and shivered. How on earth could she have got herself into such a mess? All those years of stepping up to save Alexa from herself had clearly addled her wits, for they were no longer children and she had ignored the gravity of exchanging identities as adults and the threat of legal repercussions. She was filled with horror at the idea that she might have inadvertently broken the law.

It hurt even more, though, to accept that her sister had known all along about the baby issue and had deliberately concealed that aspect because she had known that Alissa would never agree to it. Obviously, Alexa had done it for the money, that extraordinary pile of cash that had tempted and finally persuaded Alexa into deceiving her own flesh and blood for the sake of profit.

While Alissa succumbed to exhaustion and tossed and turned her way through uneasy dreams for what remained of the night, Sergei was thinking. The fire of his anger, chilled and steadied by several hours of frustrating consultation with his lawyers, was still liberally laced with outrage. He had begun to believe in Alissa, he registered in sardonic disbelief. He, who had not trusted a woman since Rozalina and who had countless experiences of female greed and dishonesty, had nevertheless mysteriously warmed to Alissa's girl-next-door warmth and seeming innocence. And yet she was clearly a fake, a lying, cheating little fake whose dazzling sex appeal just so happened to have stopped him dead in his tracks.

Her sins and his oversights had come home to roost and he had to forge a new path to his goal or he would lose everything. Losing was never an option for Sergei. He could not even contemplate such a demeaning conclusion. He studied his bruised knuckles with hard dark eyes. Some time during the night, when the endless wrangling of the lawyers during conference calls had breached his tolerance level, he had punched the wall in frustration, but now ice-cold logic was ruling him once again. He had no plans to lose *anything*, least of all the right to keep his ravishingly sexy wife in the marital bed.

When the maid entered the room and opened the curtains the next morning to let wintry daylight flood in, Alissa came awake immediately. She had a headache and a jarring jumpy sense of stress that was new to her. The very first thing she did was text Alexa, warning her twin that Sergei knew the truth and that they needed to talk urgently. Breakfast was served to her while she sat frozen in place against the pillows, recalling that ghastly confrontation with Sergei during the night.

A bitter laugh bubbled in her throat when she remembered her dizzy introspection during that candlelit bath. Hands up who was impressed to death by the gorgeous Russian billionaire who had swept her to the altar! She had sat in that bath with a diamond and emerald pendant worth thousands still clasped round her neck and she had eaten handmade chocolates while nourishing romantic ideas and feelings that could only make her shudder in retrospect. Of course she was not falling in love with Sergei Antonovich! Of course she did not admire him!

He might be her every fantasy come true in bed, but that did not excuse her for getting so carried away with her role that she had started acting like a real bride on her wedding night. Shame sat like a brick at the foot of her throat and strangled her appetite at source. At some stage, she dimly appreciated, all sense of reality had forsaken her and she had forgotten that she was virtually an employee hired to do a specific job.

And now she knew that it was a job she could never, ever fulfil. Sergei had been willing to pay a fortune for a discreet woman, willing to give him a child and then walk away without any hassle. What did that say about him? Her soft mouth trembled and she dug her fingers tightly into her palms. Not a guy who thought much of a woman's maternal instincts or even of a child's need for a mother. Not a guy who thought much of women as decent people full stop, she reckoned painfully. And all *she* had done was give him even more justification for his cynical attitude towards her sex!

Her eyes stung with tears and she blinked rapidly and sniffed, furious that her emotions were still out of her control. But she really did feel wretched and ashamed at what she had let herself get involved in. She was thinking about the man who had impassively admitted putting his alcoholic mother to bed every night as a child. Even his loving grandmother had not managed to alter Sergei's bleak view of family life. He'd had dreadful parents. And one bad marriage had evidently ensured that he was not prepared to give any woman a second chance.

Certainly not one who had already been exposed as a liar and a cheat, Alissa told herself doggedly. She mopped her face and blew her nose and struggled to pull herself back together to deal with life as it was, not as she would have liked it to be.

The phone rang while she was getting dressed.

It was not her sister as she had hoped, but Sergei. 'I'll see you downstairs in twenty minutes,' he informed her.

Alissa anchored her hair in a ponytail and stonily studied her reflection. She hadn't bothered with make-up and had pulled on jeans and a sweater. Her *own* clothes, not the borrowed glamour of the designer garments that Sergei had purchased for her. The transformation was complete and she looked ordinary again. But what was the point of gilding the lily for his benefit? Surely that would only make her feel as if she were still trying to pretend to be her more fashionable twin? She checked her mobile phone. Alexa had still not responded to her text. Impatient to talk to her sister, Alissa rang her direct and had to leave a message when the call wasn't answered.

'*Dobraye utra*…good morning.' Sergei surveyed his bride with sardonic cool when she appeared in the doorway of the elegant library he used as an office. 'Are the jeans your equivalent of sackcloth and ashes? I'm not impressed.'

Stung by his acerbic mockery, Alissa folded her arms in a defensive movement. Her struggle to maintain her composure was not assisted by the truth that, while her troubled sleep had left her pale and drawn with heavy eyes, Sergei looked as breathtakingly handsome and vibrant as a man who had enjoyed a full eight hours of undiluted rest. The leap of attraction and erotic response that slivered through her treacherous body mortified her pride. 'I hardly think that what I wear today makes any difference,' she said flatly. 'I don't feel that those clothes you bought are rightfully mine and that I should wear them.'

'Such a little puritan…' Sergei released a derisive sound of amusement that grated against her nerves in the tense silence. 'Let me see—you can marry me in a church in front of hundreds of people and allow me the freedom of your beautiful body, but your principles are too fine to allow you to wear the clothes I bought you?'

As he spoke a deep flush of humiliation slowly rose below Alissa's pale skin and washed up over her face, highlighting the sea-blue shade of her beautiful eyes. She was squirming. 'I didn't mean it like that—'

'Oh, I think you did but, as I have discovered, there's often a wide gulf between your principles and your actual behaviour.'

'Is this why you asked me to come down here? Just so that you can insult me some more?'

Sergei elevated an ebony brow. 'I don't do small talk. Or were you expecting praise for what you've done?'

Alissa drew in a sharp little breath and held it before shaking her head in grudging agreement on that point. Her gaze evaded his.

Satisfied to have put her out of countenance, Sergei lounged back against the edge of his desk to study her. Dressed like a teenager with her face bare of cosmetic enhancement, she looked outrageously youthful and innocent. He paid no heed to the aura of shame and worry that clung to her, for he was in no mood to trust such a show. He was no longer surprised that she had contrived to fool him. The greatest misogynist would have been challenged to pick her out as the calculating con artist she was, he conceded grimly. Hadn't he been taken in? Hadn't his lawyers been fooled by her sister? And hadn't he wanted Alissa so much that he had stifled his misgivings and cancelled the background check that would certainly have revealed that she was one half of a matching pair?

'What we both need to know now is—where do we go from here?' Sergei spelt out.

'I couldn't possibly meet the terms of that contract!' Alissa shot at him in a nervous rush. 'I had no idea that conceiving a child was part of the agreement. I was willing to act as your wife—'

'And share my bed with enthusiasm,' Sergei inserted silkily. 'Let's not forget that angle.'

Alissa flung her head back, her golden ponytail bouncing, her eyes very bright and reproachful. 'That just happened, for goodness' sake!'

Sergei dealt her an unimpressed look as hard as polished steel. 'In this scenario that is very difficult to believe. Sex oils so many wheels. When a man wants a woman he's more careless about the little things that don't add up.'

'Look, stop trying to make everything worse than it already is. I didn't use sex to *do* anything! I may have slept with you and I wish I hadn't,' she declared heatedly, 'but let's leave it at that. What are you going to do about all this?'

'If I do what my lawyers want me to do, I will prosecute you and your sister for fraud. One word of complaint from me and Alexa will be arrested. It is a criminal offence to deliberately sign a contract to defraud anyone of their hard-earned cash.'

Alissa met his contemptuous dark golden eyes in a horror-stricken collision. 'You *can't* do that!'

'I think you'll find that as the wronged party in this set-up I can do whatever I like.'

Desperation assailing her, Alissa was thinking frantically hard. 'But you wanted discretion and if you start prosecuting people it'll get into the newspapers. Surely you can't want that to happen?'

Sergei was impressed by the speed with which she had brandished her only possible weapon. 'Why should I care? Yelena doesn't read newspapers and it is very unlikely that anyone close to her would find out about a legal case taking place in the UK. I have done nothing wrong and nothing that I am ashamed of and publicity, bad or otherwise, isn't a matter of concern to me. Throwing you and your sister to the wolves on the other hand would at least give me some satisfaction.'

Alissa was paralysed to the spot by that blunt speech. Stone cold fear chilled her tummy, for she knew he was capable of launching a prosecution. Hard enough, vengeful enough, ruthless enough to hit back hard and hurt. Her mind kept on dropping stupidly back to the candlelit bath and the chocolates and the change in him cut through her like a knife. The day before might never have been.

'But nothing would satisfy me quite as much as the fulfilment of the original contract, *milaya moya*,' Sergei informed her smoothly. 'You assure me that that is out of the question, but tight corners have a habit of pushing back the boundaries of what people find acceptable—'

'Nothing you could do or say would persuade me to give up my own child!' Alissa snapped back at him with not an ounce of hesitation.

'I will make you an offer, then. If the money is returned in full and you agree to maintain the marriage for at least a year, I will put all thought of contacting the police on hold for the moment.'

Return the money? Of course he would want the money back, a little voice cried inside her head. She shifted position uneasily. 'From what I understand, a fair proportion of it has already been spent—'

'From what you understand?' Sergei repeated very drily. 'Are you trying to tell me that you don't have access to that money?'

'Alexa has it, but obviously I'll speak to her.'

Sergei surveyed his bride with burning disbelief. 'Your sister set up the scam, took the money and left you to deliver on the contract and face the music? And you let her do that to you? Evidently I got the dim twin, rather than the cunning, greedy one!'

Highs spots of colour burnished Alissa's cheeks. 'It wasn't like that. I'll admit that Alexa can be reckless and extravagant but she's *not* a thief—why won't you listen to me?'

'You've yet to say anything that either makes sense or is of interest to me.'

'There was no scam!' Alissa proclaimed in fierce protest.

'Then what was it? Where's my money? Or alternatively where's the woman I believed had signed a binding contract with me?' he countered harshly. 'Your sister used your name, backed out last minute and took off with the cash. You're the only hostage I've got. Isn't it time that you stopped disclaiming all responsibility and accept that you're in this up to your throat?'

In receipt of that blistering advice, Alissa swallowed hard and painfully. A tension headache was tightening like a band of steel round her brow. 'I'll try to get the money back—'

'I don't want "try", I want *will*,' Sergei emphasised. 'And don't try selling anything I've given you to pay me back with my own money.'

Alissa stiffened even more at that warning. 'I wouldn't do that. I know you probably won't believe me but I'm not a dishonest person.'

Sergei subjected her to an astringent appraisal. He was wondering if it was possible that her sister had duped her as easily as she had evidently duped his lawyers. He could see that Alissa was still in shock. He could see that she hadn't slept well. He could see that she was trembling and upset. His angular jaw line clenched and he averted his attention from her slight figure. He would have no pity for anyone who cheated him. She was in shock because she was being called to account and distressed because she feared punishment. And naturally she would want to awaken his sympathy.

Sergei straightened to his full commanding height. 'Do not doubt that I am prepared to bring the police into this.'

'I don't doubt it. But you did say that you wanted me to agree to stay as your wife for the next year,' she reminded him anxiously.

'I refuse to upset Yelena with the immediate break-down of our marriage,' Sergei said coldly.

'Okay…I'll stay,' Alissa mumbled, feeling that it was the least she could do in the circumstances.

'My priorities have changed, though.' Sergei studied the faithful fit of her sweater over the swell of her rounded breasts before raising his darkly appreciative gaze to the wide soft fullness of her mouth. Desire was already roaring through him like a hurricane force and he marvelled at the reality that he wanted her as fiercely now as he had wanted her before he had consummated their marriage. He was amazed by her continuing pull on his libido.

'How?'

'I want you in my bed whenever I want you, and with no more nonsense about not wanting to be with me.' Sergei lifted his arrogant dark head high, his glittering golden eyes hurling a challenge. 'If I'm not going to get a child out of this arrangement, that will be my compensation.'

Aquamarine eyes wide with alarm at that bold demand, Alissa was wildly aware of the burning heat of his sensual scan of her body and she slowly turned a painful pink shade.

'And that is not negotiable in any way,' Sergei intoned soft and low. 'I will only let you go free if you return that money.'

Alissa sent him an anguished look. 'I couldn't just go on sleeping with you as though nothing has happened!'

Sergei shrugged a broad shoulder in a show of outrageous nonchalance. 'I think you'll find you can, just like you did yesterday when you were the only one of us aware of the deception,' he reminded her with a sardonic curl to his handsome mouth. 'I'm leaving for London in an hour but you're staying here.'

'Why?'

'I'm giving you three days to decide what your next move will be. And if you're staying on my terms, I expect you in my bed waiting for me when I get back, *milaya moya*.'

Incensed by that cutting little speech, Alissa took a hasty step forward.

Sergei reached for her in almost the same movement. He hauled her bodily into his arms and tasted her parted lips with a hot, driving hunger that took her by shock and storm. She shivered against his unyielding masculine contours, her straining breasts crushed by his powerful torso, a firestorm of response flaring like a shameless fever in her pelvis and leaving her legs weak.

'I think that after you've considered your position you'll make it a honeymoon to remember, *angil moy*,' Sergei breathed in a tone of strong satisfaction.

Her fingers crept up to touch her tingling swollen mouth. 'A honeymoon?' she echoed blankly.

'On my yacht, where we'll have perfect privacy. *Smile*,' Sergei urged with sudden raw impatience, exasperated by her lack of enthusiasm. 'Giving you a choice between a prison sentence and my bed is very generous of me, more generous than you deserve.'

And Alissa saw that he did indeed believe that her apparent wrongdoing fully excused him for using the most unscrupulous tactics against her. She also knew better than to call Sergei's bluff. He wasn't joking. He wasn't making empty threats. He would be within his rights if he made an official complaint to the police through his lawyers. She pictured her pregnant sister being arrested and charged, closely followed by herself. As the prime instigator, Alexa might well receive the heavier punishment, but what consolation would that be to either of them? The same cold fear infiltrated Alissa again. She *had* to persuade her sister to return the money she had received for signing that contract.

'Why did you want a baby? Just to make Yelena happy?' she asked Sergei on impulse as she turned to leave the room.

Sergei glanced at her in surprise. 'That was my main motivation when I first came up with the idea,' he admitted. 'But I do genuinely like children and I would like a worthy cause to work for, other than myself.'

Alissa went upstairs and phoned her sister again. When she received no response she called her mother instead and found herself having to talk at length about her wedding and the guest lists for the London party her mother was eagerly planning before she could ask how to get in touch with her twin.

'That could be a problem,' Jenny Bartlett replied ruefully. 'Harry and Alexa are staying in a Turkish villa and she told me not to expect her to ring.'

That night Alissa lay in bed thinking about Sergei, who wanted a family of his own even though he wouldn't admit it in those terms. *A worthy cause to work for, other than myself.* In the darkness she blinked back tears and wondered what on earth she was going to do and whether it would be possible for her to go on sharing a bed with Sergei without getting emotionally involved. She was convinced that eventually he would wake up to the awareness she was really nothing that special and his desire for her would die.

For the first time she was remembering that Sergei and his lawyers had chosen Alexa to be his wife, not Alexa's more ordinary twin sister. Alexa was the sophisticated, witty twin, the one the men always went for in Alissa's experience. How long would it be before Sergei suspected that he had been short-changed in the most basic way of all with a woman who could not equal his original choice? It was a very long time before Alissa got any sleep...

CHAPTER EIGHT

'So what's all the fuss about?' Alexa demanded sulkily down the phone.

After a wait of almost thirty-six hours for a return call in response to her many messages, Alissa was so relieved to hear her twin's voice on the line that she felt momentarily dizzy and sank down heavily on the side of the bed while she spoke to her. 'For goodness' sake! Sergei has found out what we did.'

'I should have known you couldn't keep your mouth shut.'

'That had nothing to do with it! How could you not tell me that having a baby was part of that contract?' Alissa snapped back, angry disgust girding every syllable of her response. 'You must have known I would never agree to anything so outrageous.'

'You said you'd do anything to help Mum. And obviously you could have taken contraceptive pills to make sure it didn't happen.'

Alissa felt a surge of disbelief at that suggestion. 'How could you let me marry Sergei on false pretences? It was a rotten thing to do! It wasn't fair to me and it wasn't fair to him either!'

'Since when did being fair to Sergei become an ambition of yours?' Alexa demanded. 'Are you trying to make brownie points at my expense?'

'You're just not taking this seriously, are you?' Alissa censured tightly. 'Sergei is very angry and he is threatening to have us both prosecuted for fraud. What you did was illegal, Alexa...'

Alexa giggled. 'He's never going to go public with a story like this! Can you imagine how embarrassing that would be for him?'

'I think you should know that Sergei doesn't embarrass easily,' Alissa inserted sharply.

'He's just trying to scare you when he makes a threat about prosecuting us, Alissa. He doesn't mean it.'

Alissa realised then that the belief that Sergei would never risk the story of that contract getting into the newspapers had always been her sister's insurance policy against retribution. 'You're wrong. He's deadly serious and he wants his money back.'

'Well, he's got no hope of that!'

'Alexa, I now know that you got a *huge* amount of money for signing that contract. You landed me into this situation and you can get me out of it again. You have to sell that car and return as much of the rest of that money as you can put together to Sergei's lawyers in London.'

'Or what?' Alexa sniped.

'You cheated him, you cheated me. Don't you feel any shame about that? Sergei kept his side of the bargain but you didn't and I *can't*. Keeping that money when you didn't earn it is the same as stealing and I'm shocked that you can't see that!' Alissa condemned angrily.

'Sergei thinks we deliberately set out to defraud him and he blames me for it. What's got into you, Alexa?'

'What's got into you? You're my sister. Where's your loyalty?'

'Loyalty doesn't come into this. You have to repay the money!'

'You're being so stupid! I can't possibly repay all that I've spent. Don't phone me again, just leave me alone— this is supposed to be my honeymoon and I'm not about to let you wreck my marriage or my bank balance with your accusations and threats!' Alexa blazed back at her in a fury and the line went dead.

Shaken by that final exchange, Alissa breathed in deep and wondered if anything she had said had hit home hard enough to influence her headstrong sister. She had not said half of what she would have liked to have said. But then it would have been counterproductive to tear too many strips off Alexa at the same time as she was striving to persuade her twin to redress some of the damage she had done. Pushed too hard Alexa would only rebel and take easy refuge in geographical distance and silence.

Alissa went downstairs for breakfast and received a personal visit from the chef, who wanted her to choose meals for the rest of the week. He was quickly followed by the housekeeper, who had several concerns to discuss with her. With one of Sergei's aides brought in to act as an interpreter, Alissa realised that she really did need to learn enough of the Russian language to make herself understood if she was going to be in St Petersburg for much longer. She picked meals without knowing what they were and agreed, after a tour of inspection, to the redecoration of a smoke-stained bedroom damaged by a guest who had fallen asleep with a cigarette in his hand. Afterwards, she fingered the heavily etched wedding ring she wore. With Sergei on her mind night and day without cessation and his household staff coming to her for instructions, she was beginning to feel as if she was really and truly married to him.

And since there was nothing further she could do at present to change her current situation, shouldn't she be doing more in one of the most scenic cities of the world than sitting behind closed doors and worrying? That decision reached, Alissa informed Borya, who suddenly seemed to be constantly hovering around her, that she wanted to go out and where. She wondered why the older man hadn't accompanied Sergei to London. Having donned a purple wool dress and a ravishing full-length coat and boots, Alissa left the house with Borya and his team in tow and commenced her sightseeing tour.

The rest of the day just vanished in the vastness of the baroque green and white Winter Palace and the State Hermitage Museum. Countless art collections were housed within the magnificent cluster of buildings that overlooked the Neva River. Alissa wandered from room to room, dazzled by the priceless works of art and fabulous antiquities on display, grateful for the distraction from her troubled thoughts. In the gardens that lay opposite, she decided that it was too cold for a walk when it began snowing. Big, fat, fluffy snowflakes were drifting down. Even though she had carefully layered her clothing and taken every precaution to keep warm, the icy air pierced her to the bone. She was hurrying back to the limousine when someone shouted her name and she stilled in surprise and spun round, only to notice the camera angled at her too late to avoid it. Borya let out a roar and two of his team set off in hot pursuit of the paparazzo. She was relieved to get back to the house, where she delighted the chef by eating a substantial meal and slept like a log through the night.

The following day, determined not to sit around awaiting either Sergei's or Alexa's next move or phone call, she set off doggedly for Peterhof, a palace complex outside the city. The park of golden statues and elaborate fountains was white with snow and the temperature chilled her to the bone. Her security team had taken the hint from the day before and wore hats and heavy overcoats. When she slept that night she dreamt of wolves chasing her through the park and the endless ornate rooms.

The afternoon of the next day, she was flown out to Sergei's yacht, which was anchored at Antibes, where the weather was considerably milder. The long sleek craft was called *Platinum* and the crew was almost entirely English. She was given a tour of the incredibly opulent vessel and the name seemed peculiarly apt for the lavish décor. The facilities ranged from a home cinema to a gym and a disco bar and sunbathing area that boasted a swimming pool. The master suite in particular was an amazing space with private terraces and seating areas and a marble bathroom of such staggering opulence that she wanted to leap straight into the bath and pretend she was Cleopatra.

As soon as she boarded the yacht set sail. After dining at a table with panoramic views of the sea, she sat down on a sofa in the master suite and switched on the evening news on the wall-hung television screen. She tensed at the sound of Sergei's name and turned up the volume. A photo of their wedding was briefly shown, followed by a view of Sergei standing at a podium in a crowded function room while half a dozen journalists shot questions at him. Evidently he had just taken over some international company. The screen then flipped to a solo shot of Alissa in the snow in St Peterburg. She frowned as she realised it had to be the picture stolen by the paparazzo who had taken her by surprise earlier. The voiceover sounded serious and indeed Sergei was—a wedding one day, big business on the other side of the world the next…and his bride abandoned to find her own amusement…

Sergei flew in to the yacht later than he had planned. His ears were still ringing from Yelena's censorious phone call an hour earlier. His grandmother had seen Alissa on television alone in the park and had been aghast that Sergei could have left his bride to her own devices so soon after the wedding. Alissa had definitely been a big hit with Yelena, Sergei conceded wryly, for never before had Yelena attempted to interfere in his relationship with a woman.

A bottle of champagne and two glasses were brought out to the terrace where Alissa was watching the sun go down. The yacht was moored off a Greek island studded with little white buildings and arrow-shaped green cypresses. The sea glimmered in the fiery glow of sundown. By the time she heard a helicopter coming in to land, darkness had fallen and only the stars lightened the heavens.

Alissa sat as stiff as a stick of rock on her comfortable sofa. Sergei hadn't even bothered to phone her to tell her he would be coming, but the incredible industry of the crew rushing about cleaning and polishing throughout the afternoon had forewarned her of his arrival. And while she wasn't demeaning herself to the level of a nonentity by waiting in bed for him as instructed, she wasn't wearing jeans and a sweater and a scrubbed bare skin either. He had not given her a choice and she was playing it safe, not least for her mother's sake for, whatever else might have gone wrong, Alissa had not allowed herself to forget that her beloved parent's future had been secured by Sergei's money.

Powered by a strong sense of anticipation, Sergei strode away from the helipad and took the private steps up to the master suite two at a time. She was on the terrace, dressed in something glamorously long and blue and silky. Her golden hair was loose on her shoulders, framing an exquisite face dominated by her lucid aquamarine eyes and the rosebud perfection of her lush mouth. His desire ignited with satisfying urgency and he smiled down at her.

After the manner in which they had parted, his unexpected smile knocked Alissa for six as it lit up his stunning dark eyes and added a bucket of compelling charisma to his arrestingly handsome features. Sergei was always such a very unpredictable force of nature, she reflected ruefully. But his sheer physical impact pinned her to her seat. Everything about Sergei was larger than life and powerful. Crackling with high-voltage energy, he towered over her, all broad shoulders and lean hips and long legs. In a sleek black pinstripe suit that had the tailored perfection of fit that flaunted expense and exclusivity, Sergei Antonovich was as stunningly good-looking as he was white-hot sexy. Something tightened low in her pelvis and her nipples lengthened into straining points. Her mouth was dry as a bone and breathing was a challenge as she stared at him.

'Champagne?' Sergei uncorked the bottle and let the golden liquid cascade down into the elegant flutes before extending one to her.

'Are we celebrating?' Alissa enquired helplessly.

Sergei quirked an ebony brow. 'You tell me. I assume your presence here means you're staying for the foreseeable future.'

Alissa thought of a dozen replies, all of which would have pointed out that she really had very little choice unless she was prepared to sacrifice pretty much her entire family's future as well as her own. But just as quickly she recalled his insistence that she stop hiding behind what he regarded as excuses rather than admit that she found him wildly attractive. When she looked back at him, an awkward little silence had fallen. Her complexion reddened and the flute between her fingers shook a little. 'Yes,' she said flatly, suppressing all her misgivings as well as the pretences she was used to hiding behind.

'Common sense has triumphed, *milaya moya*,' Sergei quipped. 'We both have need of each other.'

Bubbles burst beneath her nose and dampened her skin as she sipped the champagne.

'But now you've deprived me of having wonderfully erotic dreams about chaining you up as a prisoner at the foot of my bed,' Sergei husked in completion, golden eyes glinting from below the luxuriant fan of his black lashes in raw sensual challenge.

Her heart hammered and her body quickened. It shook her that the very idea of being a prisoner in Sergei's bedroom roused a response from her body that she could not stifle.

'I've thought of nothing else,' he confided, sinking down beside her and setting his champagne flute down.

'Since you went away you've done nothing but eat, sleep and breathe business.' Alissa could not resist making that contradiction.

'The faster I closed the deal, the sooner I could return. You're the only reward I wanted,' Sergei told her thickly, pulling her to him to taste her ripe mouth with a warm sensual pressure enlivened by the deeply erotic dart and thrust of his tongue. Her fingers sank deep into his black hair while her senses leapt into awareness and she moaned beneath that onslaught.

While he kissed her, he let his hand roam over her silk-encased length, lingering on the firm swell of her breasts and the prominence of her taut nipples. Soon little responsive sounds trapped in her throat were escaping and she was trembling on the edge of an excitement so intense she feared it. With a hungry groan, he hoisted her up into his arms and strode indoors.

'Would I need to chain you up?' Sergei asked thickly, standing her between his spread thighs and lifting the robe she wore to explore the quiveringly ready body concealed beneath.

She could barely breathe for excitement but she had not forgotten his forecast that some day she would be as clingy and adoring as his other lovers. 'Yes, you would,' she told him even as she let her head fall back and her lips part on a helpless whimper of response as his thumb rubbed her clitoris and his skilled fingers probed the hot slippery heart of her femininity, sending delirious waves of delight pounding through her as wildly as breakers on a beach.

'*Patse luy min-ya*…kiss me,' he commanded roughly, lifting her and bringing her down on the edge of the table.

And, wanting his mouth again, she did as he asked and rejoiced in his passion. The wood of the table was cool beneath her overheated skin but she didn't care. She was pulling at his belt, wanting, needing with a strength that came close to pain. Sergei brushed aside her fingers and dealt with the clasp that had defeated her. With a guttural groan of relief and pleasure, he finally drove his engorged length into her hot damp sheath. A drowning, dizzying rush of honeyed sweetness and excitement surged through her as every sensation forced her closer and closer to a rapturous climax.

'Don't stop…*don't* stop!' she gasped wildly.

Holding her tightly to him, he pounded into her tender core with spellbinding passion. And when she went into orgasm, it was like a massive firework display going off inside her, her entire body burning and soaring with the all-encompassing high of ecstasy. The languor and peace of satiation finally followed.

'I can never get enough of you, *angil moy*,' he breathed raggedly into her hair, turning up her face to steal a scorchingly possessive kiss from her lips while smoothing her tumbled hair back from her damp brow and studying her with smouldering dark eyes. 'One minute after I come I want you again.'

Little tremors and aftershocks of pleasure were still quaking through Alissa's slight body. She was shattered by the force of need he had awakened in her and the mind-blowing pleasure he had given her. As the intense sensation faded she was aghast at the reality that he had enjoyed her on top of a table while still fully dressed. She watched him as he impatiently shed his clothes in an untidy heap.

'Aren't you ever tidy?' she sighed.

'I have more important things to do. But you're talking like a wife,' he commented in surprise and he laughed, dark golden eyes suddenly glinting with amusement.

'Isn't that what you want?' Alissa traded, lifting her chin.

'*Da*…yes. I want the full package. But right now we need a shower,' he told her, peeling the robe she wore off before he gathered her up into his arms.

'I can't give you the full package,' Alissa reminded him in an anxious warning. 'Don't you dare try to get me pregnant.'

Sergei frowned. 'Not without your consent. I've used a condom every time I've been with you…except the first time,' he mused, startling her with that admission. 'That was before I knew who you were and there seemed no point in taking precautions when the ultimate goal was a child.'

As Sergei lowered her down to stand on her own feet in the spacious shower Alissa was pale and tense. She had assumed that he had protected her the first time as well. She had been so out of control that she hadn't noticed and she was furious that she had failed to look out for herself. 'Let's hope we get away with it,' she remarked in a brittle voice.

'I was expecting it to take at least a year for you to

conceive and the last thing I would want is for that to happen now, when we no longer have either an understanding or an agreement in place. Of course, as you get to know me better, you may well change your mind on that issue—'

'No way!' Alissa asserted fiercely. 'I won't change my mind. A child needs a mother and my child will need me—'

'You're so sexist, *angil moy*,' Sergei censured, pulling her into the path of the multi sprays of water, laughing without reserve when she yelped as a needle-sharp spray hit a sensitive spot. He hoisted her up against him, her arms coiling round his neck as he braced her hips against the marble wall and wrapped her legs round his waist. 'What would you do with my baby? Use it as a weapon against me? Would you keep us fighting never-ending custody battles and constantly up the stakes to feather your own nest while hitting out at me?'

'Is that what you think women do?'

'I've watched a lot of my friends go through hell over access to their children by former partners. Even marriage is no protection. It's not a situation I will put myself or my child in with any woman. Women often want revenge when a relationship breaks down.'

Shocked by the strength of his opinions on the subject, Alissa just shook her head slowly. 'I would just love my baby and no matter what happened I would try to base all my decisions on what was best for my child.'

His lean dark features clenched hard. 'You say all the right things, *milaya moya*. You said them to your sister on the phone as well but unfortunately you don't always seem to live up to them.' He released her and strode out of the shower.

Alissa took a moment or two to get her thoughts straight and then raced after him to yell, 'How the heck do you know what I said to my sister on the phone?'

'I had your calls monitored. I wanted to know if you were telling me the truth.'

Alissa gave him an appalled appraisal. 'You had them monitored—you *snooped* on me? That's a dreadful thing to do!'

'Unlike you I didn't lie, cheat or set out to defraud anyone,' Sergei responded drily. 'You can always trust me to give you the truth, but I will not be kept in the dark about anything that concerns my interests.'

Belatedly becoming aware of the chilly evening air striking her wet, dripping body, Alissa coloured and dived back into the bathroom for a towel. While she dried off her damp hair she struggled to recall what she had said to Alexa during that phone call and cringed at the awareness that Sergei must have heard every word. He was watching the business news when she reappeared. Ignoring him, she wriggled into silk pyjamas and got into bed.

'Are we actually going to share the same bed all night?' Alissa demanded abruptly. 'I thought you didn't do couple-type stuff.'

Sergei ran an appreciative hand down over the curve of her hip as she lay there with her back turned to him. 'You've taught me to see advantages I never saw before. For the next few weeks we are going to share everything like normal newly marrieds.'

But Alissa could not understand the reasoning behind

that decision. If she was not about to give him a child what was the point of greater familiarity? And surely so much intimacy was not required to make their marriage look real from the outside? From what she could work out they were unlikely to see enough of his grandmother for there to be any need to put on such a show of being close.

'Stop agonising over everything. So, you're not perfect, but then I never expected you to be and my desire for you makes me more tolerant,' Sergei murmured with unnerving intuition. 'Relax, close your eyes, go to sleep.'

And somehow she did, waking at some stage of the night to find that she was closely entwined with Sergei's lean muscular body and far too close to him for comfort. Her squirming efforts to ease free without waking him roused him very thoroughly in a way she had not intended and her pyjamas did not last long as a barrier. Exhaustion kept her asleep until dawn when once again the touch of his expert hands on her sinfully sensitised body set ripples of tormenting need loose inside her and tightened every nerve ending to screaming point. When he finally entered her, slow and deep and sure, the breath left her body in a hiss of reaction and the flood of sweet, painfully intense sensation engulfed her. The yearning was more than she could bear and all control fell away as he sent her hurtling headlong into the burning, melting waves of irresistible satisfaction.

Afterwards, she twisted round in his arms and buried her face in a broad bronzed shoulder, breathing in the scent of his sweat-dampened skin as if it were the elixir of life while she hugged him close. Her body wasn't her own any more; when he touched her she could not resist him. That scared her. Too much exposure to Sergei was bad for her. She felt clingy, which appalled her, and she had no intention of letting that urge out to cause havoc with her self-discipline. She only hoped she wasn't pregnant, for she did not share his apparent conviction that one act of lovemaking without protection was insufficient for conception. And that was one complication they could certainly do without....

CHAPTER NINE

'*Ty v poryadka?*… Are you okay?'

A frown of annoyance mingled with concern stamped on his lean bronzed face, Sergei hovered on the threshold of the bathroom, held back only by Alissa's frantic hand signals warning him to keep a distance. 'Look, I'm calling a doctor. I think you've caught a bug.'

'I don't need a doctor,' Alissa protested, freshening up at the sink, her voice rather shrill because with every day that passed her anxiety was steadily mounting. Her period was well over a week late, her breasts were sore and attacks of nausea were making her throw up without good reason at odd times of the day. She had already worked out which diagnosis she most feared.

Ignoring her objections, Sergei got on his phone to arrange for a doctor to be brought out to the yacht as soon as possible. Alissa was a sickly green colour and he was convinced that she had succumbed to some ongoing bug or infection. He stared down at Mattie, the little scruffy dog frantically wagging his stub of a tail and licking at his shoes. He finally bent down to give Mattie a reassuring pat to prevent him from demanding attention from Alissa, who was clearly in no fit state to respond to needs other than her own.

Over three weeks had passed since Alissa had been ashore and had first seen the dog lying injured in the gutter. One minute she had been by Sergei's side looking in the window of a gold merchant in Corfu town and the next she had been racing across the busy road at great risk to her own safety and getting down on her knees to attend to the dog. A trying day for Sergei had followed while Mattie was treated by the local vet and identified as a stray and therefore homeless. In spite of a visit to an animal sanctuary, where Sergei had made a very generous donation, Mattie, with his three legs, his tatty coat and perennially anxious expression, had somehow contrived to move in with them on the yacht. Now as Mattie cried anxiously for Alissa in the doorway Sergei sidestepped the little animal to scoop up his wife and carry her back to the bed in spite of her vehement protests.

'Just lie there, *angil moy*,' Sergei instructed, out of all patience with her independence. 'Stop being so stubborn! You're sick and you should rest.'

In truth it was a relief for Alissa to lie down in comfort and close her eyes for a few moments. She still felt dizzy and nauseous, and she was torn between exasperation at her physical weakness and dismay that she might have fallen pregnant by a man who wanted to have a child and raise it *without* her.

Sergei surveyed the pallor of her face and the slightness of her body in the bed. He was convinced she had lost weight and her healthy appetite had noticeably dwindled. He was genuinely worried about her. Possibly he was guilty of having made her overdo things. She looked fragile and he should have been treating her accordingly. But being selfish came naturally to him, he acknowledged grudgingly, and he had insisted she go swimming and waterskiing most days. When Sergei cut his working hours his unlimited energy needed the outlet of physical activity. In and out of bed, theirs had been a very active honeymoon. He had taken her everywhere with him, regardless of the reality that she was no more into fishing than she was into football. On the other hand, he reflected abstractedly, she could add an excitement to a picnic in a deserted cove that no fish alive or dead could have delivered.

'I'm being a real drag,' Alissa sighed, fighting back her fatigue even to speak. 'I bet your last honeymoon wasn't like this.'

'Most days Rozalina was far from sober or nursing a heavy hangover and she stayed in bed until nightfall,' Sergei countered with unhidden distaste. 'You feeling off colour occasionally is nothing.'

Alissa had pushed herself up on her elbows to study him with bemused eyes. 'Didn't you appreciate that she was a heavy drinker when you married her?'

'I didn't notice. I was only twenty-two and the marriage was a joke. She was a party girl round the clock and it got on my nerves even before the honeymoon was over.'

'I can imagine,' Alissa murmured. She had noticed his caution with alcohol and he never drank very much. After his experiences with an alcoholic mother, a wife who couldn't stop drinking would have been a serious turn-off for him.

'Your addiction to chocolate is a lot easier to live

with, *milaya moya*,' Sergei quipped, looking so aston-
ishingly handsome as his sensual mouth curved into a
charismatic smile that her heart skipped a startled beat.

A middle-aged doctor was collected at the harbour
and brought out to the yacht within the hour. When
Sergei showed worrying signs of wanting to stay for the
consultation, Alissa persuaded him to leave. She wasted
no time in telling the doctor that she thought she might
be pregnant, but that she preferred to keep that private
if he decided that her suspicions were correct. After an
examination and an on-the-spot test, he was able to give
her that confirmation and, even though she had thought
she was prepared for that news, the acknowledgement
that she had indeed conceived Sergei's child left her in
a state of shock.

Sergei rejoined her and shifted his lean brown hands
in a gesture of frustration. 'The doctor said the sickness
would go away and that there's nothing to worry about.
Shouldn't he have prescribed something for you to take?'

'I'm not that sick...maybe I've just got a little run-
down,' Alissa suggested, swinging her legs off the side
of the bed and gathering up the panting bundle of dog
that hurled itself ecstatically at her knees. 'Mattie's so
affectionate, isn't he? He just loves to be fussed over. You
can tell that he's never had so much attention before.'

Sergei watched Mattie turn up his tummy to be
tickled and suppressed a sigh. She was more concerned
about the dog than about her own health. 'Stay in bed
for a while—get some sleep,' he urged, snapping his
fingers to bring the dog darting back to his heels as he
left the suite.

A baby, Alissa thought in wonder, checking her

still-flat tummy in a mirror while she ignored Sergei's advice and got dressed. Sergei's baby…that he wouldn't want to share. He didn't trust her sex and she had given him good reason not to trust her. What was she supposed to do now? When it occurred to her that out of distrust he might try to take her child away from her she just wanted to run and keep on running away from him.

And feeling like that was a great shame, she acknowledged heavily, after such a long happy run spending over three weeks together on board *Platinum*. In truth, she had become very deeply attached to Sergei, but nothing would have elicited that admission of deep love and even stronger caring from her. She had got so used to being with him…the sudden explosions when anything went wrong…the immense satisfaction when things went right. Without a doubt Sergei was a volcanic personality, but he absolutely fascinated her and he could make the most ordinary pursuits entertaining.

When had she reached the stage that she would sneak down to look through the glass wall of his office just to get a look at him while he spent several hours away from her to catch up with business? When the sight of him lying asleep by her side in the early hours could turn her heart inside out? Or when a glimpse of him covertly petting Mattie could make her eyes smart with stupid tears? He hadn't wanted the little dog at all at first and had been astonished when she had failed to leave the injured animal to recuperate at the sanctuary. But, day by day, Alissa had watched Mattie limping and hopping valiantly out of his basket to steadily wear down Sergei's defences and wheedle his way into full acceptance. It was becoming more and more of a challenge to keep her emotions under control around him.

But normal life was about to intervene. It was the last full day of their honeymoon and she was already wondering ruefully when she would next have Sergei all to herself. He had not yet told her when they would be leaving but *Platinum* was cleaving through the waves at a purposeful pace far different from the idyllic lazy cruising that had distinguished their exploration of the Greek islands.

She had spoken to Prince Jasim's wife, Elinor, several times in recent weeks. She had enjoyed catching up with news about Elinor's life and children and had found it a comfort to be able to chat to her friend, even though she had not felt able to confide fully in her.

'Where are we?' Alissa queried, peering through the salon windows at the picturesque harbour when the yacht dropped anchor late afternoon.

'It's a surprise. Are you sure you're well enough to go ashore?' Sergei prompted.

'I'm great...' Alissa executed a twirl, golden hair rippling in the sunlight, her purple sundress splaying round her slim figure. She was making a real effort to hide her tension and the growing fear that her only option was to walk out on Sergei before he realised that she had already conceived his child. Even he had admitted that he did not want that to happen without a legal agreement in place between them. And yet, in spite of those anxieties, Alissa was also experiencing an inner glow of awe and pleasure when she thought about the baby growing inside her womb.

They disembarked from the yacht at the busy marina

where a Turkish customs officer stamped their passports and a four-wheel-drive awaited them.

'I had no idea we would be visiting Turkey,' she told Sergei as the vehicle hurtled through busy noisy streets before climbing into the lush green hills studded with villas.

'Didn't it occur to you that we weren't that far away from the Aegean coast?'

'No, geography was never my strong point. Sergei, where on earth are we going?' she demanded, desperate to know what the surprise was.

'To see your sister and her husband,' Sergei revealed.

Alissa, who had already considered and dismissed that possibility, spluttered, 'You can't be serious!'

'I've got to meet Alexa some time. Why not now?'

'But she's pregnant,' Alissa protested vehemently. 'She mustn't be upset.'

Sergei gave her a surprised glance. 'She's not pregnant any more. I assumed your mother would have told you but perhaps she doesn't know yet either?'

Alissa stared at him in consternation. 'Alexa's lost her baby—how did you find that out?'

'Harry told me. Your mother gave me his number and I've spoken to him a couple of times to arrange this meeting. Your sister doesn't know we're coming. Alexa's been what Harry calls…temperamental and I think he's hoping that seeing you will improve her mood.'

Outside a smart white villa with a glorious view of the marina and the sparkling Aegean waters far below, Alissa climbed out. She was as taut as a bowstring. The sun was warm on her shoulders and, with her heart heavy at the news that her sister had lost her baby, she was keen to see Alexa and offer what comfort she could. 'You can't say anything about that contract or the money,' Alissa warned Sergei anxiously. 'Promise me you won't say anything because Harry knows nothing about the whole business.'

Sergei nodded acquiescence with an inhuman cool that made Alissa even more suspicious and on the alert. He had breathed fire like a dragon over Alexa's deception, yet now he was being calm and non committal. A stockily built attractive man with fair hair, Harry ushered them out to a shaded terrace where Alexa was reclining on a lounger. Her twin gave them a stunned appraisal and then she leapt up with a delighted smile. 'Alissa…I don't believe it!'

Alissa managed to say how sorry she was about the baby in an undertone before Alexa switched her attention straight to Sergei. Alissa watched as her twin relaxed into surprisingly copious giggles when Sergei said something droll and her tension began to evaporate. In turn she made an effort to talk to Harry.

'How has she been?' she asked.

'This is the brightest I've seen her,' Harry revealed. 'I hoped that seeing you would do the trick. I know how close you girls are.'

But Alissa could only be disturbed by the reflection that times had changed and she no longer felt so close to her twin. Although she felt as though too much water and too much hurt had gone under the bridge, her strongest urge was still a wish to ease her sister's pain over the loss of her baby. She had also decided that she would not mention her own pregnancy in case it proved too distressing a reminder for Alexa of the child she had miscarried.

CHAPTER TEN

ALEXA wasted no time in curving a managing arm round Alissa to march her indoors for a private chat. 'If we're heading out on the town tonight I need to get changed.'

'Sergei says the yacht club down at the marina isn't that fancy.'

'Don't you know that the yacht club is *the* place to be seen? It's where all the rich yachties and celebrities hang out. They're calling Bodrum the new St Tropez,' Alexa informed her drily. 'My goodness, you've been putting on the weight, haven't you?'

'Do you think so?' Alissa, who had not stepped on a set of scales in many weeks, gave her figure an anxious inspection in the mirror and belatedly noticed the way her breasts seemed to swell even in the comparatively modest neckline she was wearing today. She wondered whether the chocolate or the baby was responsible. 'Sergei likes curves,' she heard herself say defensively.

'Oh, men always say that when you ask them,' Alexa retorted with derision. 'But when they dump you, they always go off with someone half your size! So, tell me, what's it like being married to Sergei?'

Alissa perched on the edge of the bed while her twin

rifled through a packed wardrobe in search of an outfit. At that leading question she went pink. She did not want to incite her sister's scorn by launching into a panoply of praise that might even include the recent development of Sergei hurling his clothes in the direction of a chair instead of the floor. 'It's easier than I expected,' she breathed stiltedly. 'But I'm more concerned about you—when did the miscarriage happen?'

'When did the...*miscarriage* happen?' Alexa repeated, turning to stare at her sister with a frown of bemusement. 'Don't be silly, Allie. That story was only for Harry's benefit. There never was a baby. I was sure you would have worked that out for yourself by now.'

Alissa stared back at the slim blonde woman in stunned disbelief, for Harry had not been the only person affected by that inexcusable pretence. Alexa had even used the threat of an abortion to pressure Alissa into taking her place as Sergei's wife. '*Never?* You were never pregnant? I'm sorry, I find that very hard to believe after some of the things you said to me.'

'It suited me to pretend I was pregnant,' Alexa told her defiantly. 'And the worse thing about all this is that now even Harry suspects that I was lying all along.'

'My word, does he?'

'After a shotgun wedding, what man wouldn't be suspicious? I told him I had had a very early miscarriage that didn't require medical attention, but I'm not sure he's convinced.'

Alissa was sincerely appalled at the ease with which Alexa had lied and misled even her own family, behaviour that did not appear to have awakened her twin to either guilt or regret. 'Why on earth did you get us all involved in your lies? How could you have wept in front of me and told me how much you longed to marry Harry and have his baby when there never was a baby?' she gasped in condemnation.

'For the money, of course!' Alexa gave her a look of scorn. 'You do ask crazy questions sometimes. Once I found out I'd have to get pregnant to fulfil that contract with Sergei, I knew there was no way I could ever face going through with it and that I would have to hand over the opportunity to you. I mean, even the thought of ruining my figure with a pregnancy turns my stomach!'

Listening to that frank confession, Alissa only contrived to hang onto her temper with the greatest difficulty. A fierce and bitter sense of betrayal gripped her at the knowledge that she could so easily have been taken in by the twin she loved and had trusted. Until Alexa had admitted the fact, Alissa had had no idea that her sister was revolted by the very concept of pregnancy. 'So all that stuff about you being pregnant was simply a lie to pressure me into marrying Sergei in your place?'

'As I said, I handed the opportunity to you, and haven't you done well out of it?' Alexa flung back without shame while she treated Alissa's appearance to a deeply envious appraisal. 'I did you a favour. A gorgeous guy with a yacht the size of the *Titanic*? A huge diamond on your finger? He never stops spending money on you—obviously you're doing something right. You've been shopping until you drop round the Greek islands with the paps dogging your every move—be honest, you're living the life most women would kill to have!'

'But I don't want Sergei because he's rich!' Alissa yelled back at her sister in a positive passion of angry distaste. 'I want him for the man he is, not for what he has. I'd want him even if he was broke!'

'I don't believe it…you've actually been stupid enough to fall in love with a guy who chose to *employ* a woman to marry him.' Alexa studied her with disdainful amusement. 'Are you insane? As far as he's concerned you're not a real wife, you're just the hired help!'

The reminder sobered Alissa as nothing else could have done, because while such words were unwelcome she recognised the truth of them in her heart. Falling for Sergei had always been a major no-no and yet she had foolishly done it. Common sense had gone out of the window the first night she'd met him. And while Sergei's forecast that she would fall in love with the game of football was still being challenged by the effort it took for her to stay awake until the end of a match, she had fallen head over heels for him almost straight away.

'And I could take Sergei off you again in five minutes,' Alexa forecast with a patronising smile. 'After all, if he finds you attractive, he'll find me positively irresistible! Would you like me to give you a demonstration?'

'I don't think you're likely to get very far with Sergei until you return that money you accepted on false pretences,' Alissa said gently, anything but amused by her twin's nasty wounding assurance that Sergei would go for her more sophisticated charms the first chance he got.

'Watch me—I'll make it well worth his while to let me keep the cash. Don't you know how to please a man yet? It all starts and ends in the bedroom,' Alexa murmured suggestively, smiling with satisfaction at her reflection as she posed and preened in front of the mirror so that the brief silver dress she wore flashed into quick-silver folds against her long slender legs.

'That's not funny, Alexa,' Alissa said tightly.

'It wasn't meant to be. If it wasn't for me, you wouldn't even be *with* Sergei. Don't forget that,' Alexa reminded her viciously.

When she was in such a mood there was never any talking to Alexa, and Alissa was grateful to get back downstairs again where the two men were chatting on the terrace. Alissa plonked herself down next to Sergei. She was feeling threatened enough by Alexa that she would throw herself bodily onto Sergei's lap in a very public demonstration of affection if he just gave her the smallest sign of encouragement. Hyper-aware of his every move, she was agonisingly conscious of the way he stared at her sister when the silver-clad blonde made her entrance.

'What do you think of Alexa?' Alissa asked, despising herself utterly for sinking low enough to pose that question to Sergei as soon as she was alone with him.

They were driving back to the marina with her sister and Harry following in their own vehicle. Dark eyes narrowing, Sergei drawled, 'She's very different from you—*amazingly* different considering that you're identical twins.'

It was not a response that Alissa could find any comfort in receiving. In her experience she had always been labelled the plumper, plainer twin, who lacked the fun, girly, sexy sparkle of the sibling ten minutes her junior. Being more clever and more popular with her own sex had never felt like a consolation when she was aware that nine out of ten men preferred girly sparkle and sexiness.

Alissa tried very hard not to be put in the shade during the evening that followed. Hugely conscious that she was carrying Sergei's child and worrying about that reality along with her very uncertain future as his wife, she discovered that stress knocked any sparkle she might have had right out of her. Long before then, however, she was being wounded by Alexa's behaviour, for her sister was flirting outrageously with Sergei.

Sergei had no need to do anything. Alexa switched on like a high-powered searchlight and focused all her attention on him. While Harry was clearly becoming more and more annoyed by his wife's provocative behaviour, Alissa was wondering unhappily if Sergei was already convinced that he had ended up with the wrong twin. Listening to the repartee zipping back and forth between them, she could tell that Sergei was very much accustomed to women like her sister. Indeed she had the hideous suspicion that if Alexa was to ask him to choose outright between them, Alexa could have walked right out of the club with Sergei, unconcerned at deserting either her sister or her new husband.

'Are you sure you don't want anything else?' Sergei prompted Alissa, who had asked yet again for a mineral water.

'Alissa's always preaching temperance at parties!' Alexa giggled, waving her sex-on-the-beach cocktail round like a fashion statement.

'I'm just not in the mood for alcohol.'

'Alissa has been unwell,' Sergei commented, brilliant dark eyes locked to Alexa's shimmering smile of indifference.

'Oh, dear, what a drag for you on your honeymoon!' Alissa exclaimed, all her sympathy angled in Sergei's direction.

The level of her discomfiture and tension was making Alissa feel horribly dizzy and nauseous again and she took refuge in the cloakroom. Was she a drag? She could not credit that her twin was making a play for Sergei right before her eyes, and Harry's. Sitting watching it from the sidelines was a uniquely painful and sobering experience, Alissa conceded wretchedly. Sergei had done nothing to shoot down Alexa's pretensions and Alissa could see that he found Alexa both attractive and entertaining. Suddenly she asked herself why she was tolerating her situation as a powerless bystander.

Wouldn't it be better to leave, bow back out of Sergei's life before everything got even more complicated? After all, she was going to have to leave sooner rather than later, in any case. Once her pregnancy began to show, Sergei would feel cheated if she wasn't prepared to hand her baby over to him. How could he feel any other way after that wretched contract? But she wouldn't deny him access to his child; she wouldn't use her baby as a weapon. No, not even if Sergei *did* take up with her sister!

Her tummy somersaulted at that horrible prospect, which she knew she would not be able to bear in long-suffering silence. Nor, she thought in anguish, would she ever be able to forgive Alexa for making a play for Sergei. Alexa knew that Alissa was in love with Sergei. Alissa was convinced that she would never, *ever* be able to forget the pain she had endured watching her sister charming Sergei before her very eyes.

Alissa made her mind up fast. Her passport was in

her handbag. She would take a taxi to the nearest airport. Withdrawing a notebook and pen from her bag, she wrote Sergei a note, telling him that he was free and that it was better for them to part while they were still friends. *Friends?* Her soft mouth down-curved. She didn't want to be his friend, but it sounded much better than telling him that working up the courage to leave him was the hardest thing she had ever done. For a moment she almost panicked about leaving Mattie and then she added a line to the note to let Sergei know that she really, *really* wanted the little dog brought back to the UK on his pet passport.

She gave the note to a waiter along with a tip, pointing out their table, and contrived to leave the club in the wake of the departure of a large party of noisy diners. She had noticed the taxi rank earlier and it wasn't far to walk. She only had sterling notes in her purse but the driver said he was happy to accept them. It took a good forty-five minutes to reach her destination and for every minute of that time she was lost in memories of Sergei and fighting the inclination to go back.

How could she go back? What would be the point? With Sergei's outlook, the news that she had conceived his child would be bad news and he would fight her for custody, she *knew* he would. On the other hand, perhaps if she stayed a little longer and talked to him she might be able to get through to him and persuade him that a happy, healthy child ideally needed two parents. Unfortunately, after watching Sergei and Alexa together, Alissa couldn't face that option. She had to get away for her own sanity, she told herself urgently.

Buying a ticket for a flight to London was straightforward, but she had quite a few hours to wait. She bought a soft drink and sat down in a café to drink it. She was so miserable she wanted to put her head down on the table and sob. Images of the ghastly dinner she had endured watching Alexa and Sergei interact kept on returning to haunt her. But hadn't that always been her fear? That she was really second best and that if Sergei had ever got the choice, it would not have been her whom he chose? The proof of that humiliating conviction was tearing her apart. She did not think she would ever be able to look at her sister again. Didn't Sergei appreciate that all Alexa really cared about was his wealth and what it could buy her? That she had the attention span of a flea when it came to men?

A shadow fell across the table surface and she lifted her head, pushing back her blonde hair from her warm brow with a weary hand. She froze when she realised that it was Sergei standing over her, dark eyes smouldering hot as a volcanic core, his lean, dark, handsome face set in angry lines.

'Why did you follow me?' she whispered fiercely. 'It's easier if you just let me go.'

'But that's the one thing I can't do,' Sergei revealed, thrusting back the chair opposite and dropping down into it with all the force of a forest tree crashing to the ground in a storm. 'I can't let you go.'

So tense that she was barely breathing, Alissa focused on him with a treacherous surge of pleasure. She had thought she might never see him again, or at least that the next time she laid eyes on him it might be in a courtroom months from now. Just those thoughts had made her feel deprived and she had started missing him the same second she'd left his side at the club.

'You have to let me go. It's time,' she told him gruffly.

'I told you I can't do it,' Sergei delivered in a roughened undertone. 'If you try to walk away from me, I'll lift you up and carry you out of here.'

'You wouldn't do that, for goodness' sake…'

'It would probably get me arrested because no doubt you would scream and shout. But I would still do it,' Sergei intoned. 'I won't stand by and let you walk out on me without fighting.'

'But why would you fight?' Alissa was so stressed she could feel the dreaded tears gathering behind her eyes, even though she was as mad with him as she was also very upset. 'Alexa's much more your type.'

Sergei studied her levelly. 'You're the clever twin. You've got to know better than that, *angil moy*. Maybe I made a mistake not spelling out my disinterest more openly this evening.'

'Your…*disinterest*?' Alissa echoed in a doubtful tone.

'But I wanted you to see exactly what your sister is like so that you won't let her take advantage of you again. Because she will try again and again to use you and I don't want that to happen.'

Alissa was frowning at a view of the interplay round that dining table that she had not considered. 'I wouldn't let Alexa take advantage of me…'

Sergei vented a sardonic laugh and gave her an expressive glance. 'I bet she's been taking advantage of you since you were children. I also bet that she was a very spoiled and selfish child, and that your parents found it easier to give in to her iron will than stand up to her. Alexa *expects* to get away with her offences.'

'Are you saying you *don't* prefer her to me?' Alissa prompted in amazement.

'I'd sooner get down and dirty with a shark. Alexa is everything I don't want in a woman and she repulses me.' Sergei grimaced. 'Exactly what would I find attractive about her? She's smothered in make-up and she dresses like a tart. She has to be the centre of attention and she has no manners. Surely you noticed the way in which she humiliated her husband this evening?' he prompted. 'That was another reason why I didn't obviously try to repel Alexa—if I pretended that I hadn't noticed how she was coming on to me it was less embarrassing for Harry.'

It was an analysis of Alexa that left Alissa bereft of speech, for she had spent most of her life feeling overshadowed by her twin's attractions and now the accepted order of things was being swept away by Sergei's bluntly offered opinions. 'I never thought of that angle,' she said numbly. 'Poor Harry—'

'That's one marriage unlikely to last long. They were fighting when I took my leave of them—even then she was blaming you for spoiling her evening and calling you a drama queen for walking out,' Sergei breathed in disgust.

'Maybe I am a drama queen.' Alissa sighed, the sturdy foundations of her resentment being destroyed with every word he spoke, because it was patently obvious even to a bitterly jealous and insecure person such as she was herself that Sergei not only wasn't attracted to her twin, but also actively disliked her.

'No. I should've appreciated that you read the situation the wrong way. Do you think we could find somewhere more private?' Sergei angled his handsome dark head in the direction of the family with noisy kids taking seats too close for comfort.

Alissa rose upright. 'Okay—where?'

'The yacht…'

Uncertainty made her frown. 'I'm not—'

'Or I carry you bodily out of here, *angil moy*,' Sergei completed, surveying her with stubborn determination.

And she knew he would, and suddenly she was laughing and the tears spilled over a little to mingle with her laughter. She sucked in a deep breath to steady her nerves as he walked her towards the exit doors. It was dark and cool outside and he shrugged out of his jacket to drape it round her bare shoulders.

'I didn't only decide to leave because of what happened this evening with Alexa,' she warned him stiffly.

'I wouldn't have gone ahead with the marriage or the contract if she had turned up that night before the wedding,' Sergei confided abruptly as he urged her into the four-wheel drive revving its engine by the kerb. 'Until I met you, I was ready to dump the project because I wasn't attracted by her photo and I didn't like what I heard in her interviews.'

'Is that the honest truth?' Alissa prompted in an urgent whisper in the rear seat.

Sergei nodded.

'So when you said that Alexa and I were amazingly different that's what you meant…'

'*Da*…yes. You had the X-factor, she didn't, *solnyshko moyo*.' Sergei closed an arm round her and drew her close.

Alissa spent most of the journey happily adjusting to

the news that Sergei had picked her, not Alexa, to marry and that he preferred her in every way. In the moonlight his lean, strong face was a brooding arrangement of light and shade, hooded eyes dark and unfathomable. She wondered how he would feel when he realised that she was carrying his child. Was that revelation likely to divide them again?

'If you leave me, I'm keeping Mattie,' Sergei told her softly. 'That note of yours was priceless. You didn't devote one line to agonising over leaving me, but you lamented leaving Mattie behind for two and a half lines!'

'You can't have him,' Alissa asserted, fearful that he would take the same attitude over their child.

'I would have let you visit him occasionally.'

They boarded *Platinum* and Mattie raced to greet their return with panting, wriggling, doggy fervour and sharp little barks. When he had quietened down, Alissa breathed in deep. 'I have something to tell you…'

Sergei spread lean brown hands wide. 'I'm waiting— just tell me!'

'I'm pregnant—that's part of the reason why I left. I just didn't see how we could possibly manage—'

'Pregnant?' Sergei swept her up in his arms in an ex- pression of exuberance that totally took her aback. Both arms wrapped round her, he gave her a wolfish smile. 'That's the best news I've ever heard…and we didn't even have to work at it! Not that having to work at it would have been a trial,' he acknowledged with an easy masculine laugh.

'You can put me down now,' Alissa advised in a daze.

'Why? So that you can put some sort of gloomy slant on this moment?' Sergei censured in full bossy mode.

'Don't you realise that the rule book on our marriage went out the window the same day I met you?'

'It wasn't a real m-marriage!' Alissa stammered that reminder as Sergei very deliberately spread a large hand across her stomach.

'How real does real have to be before you will believe in it?' Sergei enquired, stretching her out full length across his lap and flipping up her dress so that he could bend his handsome dark head and press his lips to the bare skin of her stomach instead. 'It's amazing to think our baby's in there.'

Alissa was frozen in place by the unpredictability of his reactions to her announcement. 'You're really pleased about the baby, aren't you?'

Sergei gave her a huge smile. 'Isn't it obvious?'

Sudden tears convulsed Alissa's throat. 'It's different for me. You married me according to a contract.'

'Which you broke,' he slotted in with amusement.

'Only a few weeks ago you were threatening to prosecute me!' she slung shrilly back at him.

'A couple of weeks back, I received background reports on you and Alexa and I didn't have to be a genius to work out that your sister has never been a nice person. I knew who to blame. You were thoughtless but there's no malice in you. I went from wanting to prosecute to giving you an extended honeymoon instead. Haven't the last few weeks we've spent together taught you anything about me?'

'Only that I don't know what you're going to do or say next!' Alissa was so worked up that she burst into tears and startled him. 'I don't even know what you want from me or if you're about to try and take my baby away from me!'

Sergei framed her face with firm hands. 'I wouldn't do anything that hurt you or the baby. I want you both together...for ever.'

'*For ever?*' Alissa gasped, tears still trickling down over her cheeks.

'For ever,' Sergei confirmed, claiming a kiss with a hungry urgency that sent an entirely new source of energy coursing through her slim body. 'Because I have feelings for you that I never thought I would have for any woman and I was overjoyed by my good taste when I heard you shouting at your sister this evening that you would want me even if I was broke!'

Alissa flushed crimson. 'Oh, my goodness, you *heard* that?'

'I heard it—the window was wide open behind the shutters. I love you,' he breathed huskily, stealing yet another kiss and an even more passionate one this time that sent her senses all reeling.

'Honestly?' she checked, scarcely able to believe that all her dreams were coming true at once.

'Honestly,' Sergei confirmed with mock solemnity.

Her fingers closed round his tie and pulled it loose. 'I'm crazy about you too,' she confided breathlessly.

Sergei carried her down the companionway to the master suite. She lay in his arms with a blissful smile. 'What made you love me?'

'The oddest things.'

'Like what?' she demanded, eager to know.

'When you told me off for shouting at the checkout attendant, it was a wake-up call. When you looked like an angel in the church on our wedding day. When you insisted I send Greek postcards to Yelena and you refused even to consider having a child and giving it away.'

'You liked that even though it meant I couldn't do what you wanted?' she queried in amazement.

'I'm naturally perverse and when you got all dirty and bloody rescuing Mattie I was even more impressed. You have a big heart and I love that side of you most of all, *angil moy*,' Sergei confided, unzipping her dress so that it fell at her feet. 'But I wasn't impressed when you ran out on me tonight without even telling me what was wrong.'

'I couldn't bear watching Alexa flirt with you—'

'I couldn't bear listening to her put you down,' he countered.

'I was scared to tell you about the baby. I sort of assumed it would end everything between us and just start up a horrible dispute about custody so I saw no point in staying to talk,' Alissa admitted ruefully.

Releasing the hooks on her bra, Sergei curved her back against his muscular chest, closed his hands to her breasts and breathed raggedly. 'I won't ever let you go. You're the woman I never thought existed, the woman I believed I would never find. When my lawyers told me to prosecute and divorce you, I ignored their advice. They thought I was insane, and love must be a kind of insanity because I didn't really care what you had done. I was too busy being grateful that I didn't get the wrong sister.'

'But you've forgiven me so much.' Overwhelmed by his generosity and understanding and the strength of his love, Alissa swivelled round in the circle of his arms. 'I really, really love you, Sergei.'

With all their defences down and their mutual joy in the baby she had conceived, they had so much to share. Alissa had never known such happiness could be hers. Sergei told her about the abortion that his first wife, Rozalina, had had without consulting him and how that discovery had led to their divorce and the loss of a good part of his wealth back then. Alissa wrapped him tight in her arms and fully understood his longing for a child, a family, a secure circle of people he could love and trust and work hard to support and spoil. They made passionate love and talked far into the early hours before Sergei decided that the honeymoon should be extended by one more week.

The next day she rang her mother just to tell her how deliriously happy she was and that she had conceived. Jenny, shaken by Alexa's recent announcement that she had lost her baby, was overjoyed by the discovery that she was going to be a grandmother after all.

Just over a year later, Alissa was putting the finishing touches to the giant Christmas tree she had had erected in the drawing room. She was humming a carol under her breath as she attached delicate baubles and ornaments to the branches.

Mattie was snoozing by the fire. Alissa and Sergei's infant daughter, Evelina, was in an equally restful mood and dozing in a baby seat. Evelina had the arresting combination of her father's luxuriant black hair and her mother's light eyes. Once Alissa had got over the nauseous phase, she had had an easy pregnancy. In every way it had been a very busy and eventful year.

They'd had a second wedding in London, for Sergei had confided that his lawyers were not one hundred per cent certain that their Russian marriage was fully legal when Alexa had forged Alissa's signature on certain documents. Alissa had fully enjoyed that ceremony and her mother had enjoyed it even more. The big glitzy party that had followed had proved to be the social event of the year. Jasim and Elinor had attended and their other friend and former flatmate, Lindy, had also put in an appearance. That had been very welcome, for neither Elinor nor Alissa had seen much of Lindy recently as the younger woman was very much focused on her small crafts business and worked long hours.

For a good deal of the year, Sergei and Alissa based their lives in St Petersburg, but they were planning to live mainly in the UK once Evelina reached the age for school. Alissa's parents had reconciled, although it had been quite a few months after her father's affair with Maggie had ended before Jenny was prepared to invite her estranged husband to move back in with her again. Alissa's father had returned the money he had been given and in turn Jenny had insisted on returning all of it to Sergei. For a while Alissa had found visiting her reunited parents rather like walking on eggshells, but time had healed the worst wounds and the older couple currently seemed to be rediscovering happiness. She had also managed to regain her former closeness with her father after Sergei had pointed out that it really wasn't fair to punish people for being less than perfect.

Unhappily she had yet to reach the same accommodation with Alexa, whose own life had admittedly suffered a number of disastrous ups and downs in recent months. After a history of violent quarrelling with Harry and his family, and having had an affair with her married boss, Alexa was now in the midst of a bitter separation. While she had flatly refused to repay the money she had accepted for signing the contract with Sergei's lawyers, she now had to fight Harry's attempt to take a good share of it off her in a divorce settlement.

'What goes around comes around,' Sergei had commented cheerfully.

Alissa had not seen much of her twin over the past year but the sisters did make a point of being pleasant to each other when they met at family gatherings, for Alissa did not want her parents upset. Alexa had also made an effort to attend Evelina's christening while avoiding getting within thirty feet of Sergei's sardonic tongue. Alissa had found it easier to forgive her twin's flaws once she'd realised that Sergei was never going to be one of Alexa's admirers. At present, her strongest hope was that Alexa would stop rating the acquisition of money above everything else in her life and appreciate what was really important.

'It's good to be optimistic,' Sergei had quipped on that score, deaf to Alissa's protests. 'But please don't introduce her to any of our single male friends. I don't want anyone putting that on my conscience.'

Yelena was a frequent visitor and was arriving the following day to share her second Christmas with them. She would stay until the Russian New Year had been welcomed in. Alissa could now speak enough of her husband's native language to make herself understood and she got on very well with her husband's grandmother. Yelena positively worshipped Evelina and seemed to have no greater happiness than to sit quietly attending to her first great-grandchild.

The slam of the front door alerted Alissa to Sergei's return and wakened Evelina and the dog. Mattie trotted over to welcome Sergei home while Evelina kicked her legs in expectation of the attention she was accustomed to receiving from her father. As the door opened Alissa felt a leap of wicked anticipation flare and she studied the tall handsome male in the doorway with loving eyes and a wide smile. She had never known until she met him that another human being had the power to give her such happiness. Sergei stowed parcels on the table, contrived to pat the dog and scoop up Evelina on his way past, tucking his daughter deftly below one arm to keep the other free to reach for his wife.

'A week without you all is a week too long, *angil moy*,' he groaned, bending his proud dark head to steal a hungry kiss from her soft pink lips. 'I'll have to keep you in bed for a month before I recover from that amount of self-denial.'

Alissa moaned a little beneath the urgency of his sensual mouth, both thrilled and embarrassed by that candid warning.

Evelina let out a cry of complaint because she was being crushed and Sergei lifted the little girl playfully aloft to study her with loving attention before lowering her and smoothing her little dark head with a gentle reassuring hand. Replacing her in her seat, he turned back to his wife.

'I even missed the dog,' he groaned. 'What have you done to me?'

Alissa linked her arms round his neck and smiled up at him. 'We missed you too…'

He kissed her again, passion stirring so that her slim body welded to the lean, hard angles of his. 'I almost forgot,' he said, freeing her to lift the parcels.

Evelina got an ingenious toy to keep her amused and Alissa got a fabulous diamond eternity ring. 'It's an expression of my love and appreciation, *angil moy*,' Sergei breathed, turning the ring at an angle so that she could see the words *'For ever'* etched in flowing script on the inside with their names.

'It's wonderful,' Alissa sighed happily sliding the ring into place beside her wedding ring. 'I'll think of you every time I look at it.'

The last parcel contained a little box with a tree ornament that bore a remarkable resemblance to Mattie, or at least a four-legged version of him. Glowing with contentment, Alissa hung the thoughtful gift on the tree. Their nanny came down to collect Evelina for her bath and Sergei and Alissa enjoyed a leisurely evening meal catching up on news. Jasim and Elinor had invited them to visit Quaram in the spring and they were looking forward to the trip. On their return they would as usual be spending Easter Day with Yelena.

When dinner was over, Sergei closed his hand over Alissa's and murmured, 'I hate leaving you but I love coming back home to you, *moyo zolotse*.'

'What are you calling me?'

'Literally? "My gold", and you are.' Sergei closed her possessively into his arms, staring down at her with brilliant dark eyes warmed with love. 'When I met you, I struck a gold mine.'

Alissa smiled up at him, touched by his sincerity and grateful for the strength of the love they shared and the joy that Evelina had given them and their families. 'I'm incredibly happy with you, too.'

'I love you, *moyo zolotse*.'

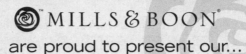

millsandboon.co.uk Community

Join Us!

The Community is the perfect place to meet and chat to kindred spirits who love books and reading as much as you do, but it's also the place to:

- **Get the inside scoop from authors about their latest books**
- **Learn how to write a romance book with advice from our editors**
- **Help us to continue publishing the best in women's fiction**
- **Share your thoughts on the books we publish**
- **Befriend other users**

Forums: Interact with each other as well as authors, editors and a whole host of other users worldwide.

Blogs: Every registered community member has their own blog to tell the world what they're up to and what's on their mind.

Book Challenge: We're aiming to read 5,000 books and have joined forces with The Reading Agency in our inaugural Book Challenge.

Profile Page: Showcase yourself and keep a record of your recent community activity.

Social Networking: We've added buttons at the end of every post to share via digg, Facebook, Google, Yahoo, technorati and de.licio.us.

www.millsandboon.co.uk

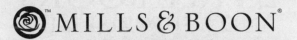

2 FREE BOOKS
AND A SURPRISE GIFT

We would like to take this opportunity to thank you for reading this Mills & Boon® book by offering you the chance to take TWO more specially selected books from the Modern™ series absolutely FREE! We're also making this offer to introduce you to the benefits of the Mills & Boon® Book Club™—

- **FREE home delivery**
- **FREE gifts and competitions**
- **FREE monthly Newsletter**
- **Exclusive Mills & Boon Book Club offers**
- **Books available before they're in the shops**

Accepting these FREE books and gift places you under no obligation to buy, you may cancel at any time, even after receiving your free books. Simply complete your details below and return the entire page to the address below. You don't even need a stamp!

YES Please send me 2 free Modern books and a surprise gift. I understand that unless you hear from me, I will receive 4 superb new books every month for just £3.19 each, postage and packing free. I am under no obligation to purchase any books and may cancel my subscription at any time. The free books and gift will be mine to keep in any case.

Ms/Mrs/Miss/Mr_____ Initials _____

Surname _____

Address _____

_____

_____ Postcode _____

Send this whole page to: Mills & Boon Book Club, Free Book Offer, FREEPOST NAT 10298, Richmond, TW9 1BR

'I expected to see you again before the wedding.'

'I'm sorry—I'd like to spend some time at home before I go to Russia.' Pale and taut, Alissa collided head-on with smouldering dark golden eyes heavily fringed with lush black lashes.

'You make it sound so reasonable, *milaya*.' Sergei reached out and closed a hand round hers as she brushed a skein of gold silky hair back from her brow. He eased her inexorably closer. 'But you know that's not what I want.'

'Surely there's some part of the day when I can have my own free time?' Alissa queried, throwing her blonde head high, a gleam of challenge in her bright eyes.

'Your own free time?' Sergei countered, his lean dark features tensing.

'Isn't this a job? I can't be on duty twenty-four-seven.'

Sergei froze, all warmth ebbing from his gaze, leaving it winter-dark and cold. 'I don't think you can have read the small print on your contract,' he breathed, in an icy, cutting tone of distaste. 'From the moment you wear my wedding ring, you *will* be on duty twenty-four-seven.'